Gone. It was all gone. The reason she sold half her wardrobe to buy a ticket all the way to Nebraska. The reason she turned down marriage to the twice-widowed butcher back in Cincinnati, Ohio. The reason she was on the ten-thirty Union Pacific to Whitewater Rapids. Now there was no reason to be there.

Wallowing in self-pity, for the first time in her life, she felt adrift without a home, a family, or anyone to care. She always had someone to take care of and be part of before. Now that her father had passed, and his professor's wages with him, Lorelei needed to find a new life for herself. This position as town librarian was to be it. Now it, too, was gone.

An Unexpected Wife

by

Susan Payne

An Unexpected Wife

Cover Art by *The Wild Rose Press, Inc.*

The Wild Rose Press, Inc.
PO Box 708
Adams Basin, NY 14410-0708
Visit us at www.thewildrosepress.com

Publishing History
First Edition, 2021
Trade Paperback ISBN 978-1-5092-3770-8
Digital ISBN 978-1-5092-3716-6

Published in the United States of America

Dedication

To my family who continue to be both my inspiration and my motivation. Especially my husband of fifty-four years.

Nebraska 1874

CHAPTER ONE

Lorelei stood facing the impressive front of the Whitewater Rapids Public Library, the tall Corinthian columns stood as sentinels to the wide, heavily carved wood doors under a gold-trimmed transom. The front palladium-styled windows with their high arches allowed the sun's rays to shine inside showing off wood paneling and space for a substantial number of desks.

The rest was a smoldering mass of charred beams and tumbled bricks. Furls of smoke meandered their way heavenward and the acrid smell of burned wood hung heavily in the air.

Soft swirls of wind caused fine ash to float in the air landing on her already travel-weary skirt and pelisse. Rivulets of tears made their way down her cheeks through the black residue covering her skin and dropped unheeded onto her once white lacy shirtwaist.

Gone. It was all gone. The reason she sold half her wardrobe to buy a ticket all the way to Nebraska. The reason she turned down marriage to the twice-widowed butcher back in Cincinnati, Ohio. The reason she was on the ten-thirty Union Pacific to Whitewater Rapids. Now there was no reason to be there.

Wallowing in self-pity, for the first time in her life, she felt adrift without a home, a family, or anyone to

1

care. She always had someone to take care of and be part of before. Now that her father had passed, and his professor's wages with him, Lorelei needed to find a new life for herself. This position as town librarian was to be it. Now it, too, was gone.

The men with hoses near the hand-pumped fire engine all seemed busy making sure they doused every ember. They did a good job saving a shell of a building, but none of the contents or left them a soggy mess. She shook her head. She needed to remember this wasn't Cincinnati with its trained firemen and expensive firefighting equipment. She would bet there wasn't a real fireman among them or a fire station nearby. But why was she angry? They had done their best, and no other buildings fell victim to the same hungry flames.

The activity in front of her eyes died down just as any sign of new life to the fire died out. She was startled when a man's voice sounded close by.

"Ma'am? May I help you with something? You seem to be crying, and I know we didn't lose anyone in the fire. Do fires remind you of a bad time in your past?"

His clothes were covered with dark streaks and smeared stains. She gazed into the smoke-smudged eyes of a tall man. Their sky blue color seemed innocuous surrounded by soot, which covered most of his skin. Blond hair showed, and she could see it had been singed where his hat hadn't protected it. He held that in his hands now, twisting the brim nervously.

Bringing her mind to the present, she shook her head. "No, no, it doesn't bring back any bad memories. Simply the loss of new ones, I guess. I am mourning something that never happened."

"Ma'am, I don't know what you're talkin' about. I'd like to help you, but I'm not sure how."

She tried to smile to lessen his feelings of guilt or whatever made him stop to help a stranger, a dirty, sooty stranger, crying in the middle of the street. "I'll be fine in a minute or two."

He seemed unsure how to proceed and pulled a handkerchief out of his pocket to hand to her. He seemed embarrassed at its condition. "Sorry, I had to use it to cover my nose and mouth when I was making sure no one was inside. What a day to leave home without a bandana, huh?"

She nodded and pulled a lace-trimmed hankie out of the cuff of one sleeve and dabbed at her eyes noting the amount of black staining the once-pristine linen. She wasn't sure how bad she appeared, but if she looked half as dirty as the man in front of her then she was a sight.

A heavyset man, wearing as dirty a suit of clothes as the cowboy, huffed up to them. "Luke, you hurt? And, ah, I'm afraid I don't recognize you beneath the soot, Ma'am, but are you hurt? Were you near the fire?"

"No, I've been here a short while, but as you said, I look as if I had been fighting the fire, as well. I am, no, I was, the librarian hired to organize and run the library." Her gaze floated over the still-smoldering building. "Now I guess I'm unemployed."

"Miss Sanders, I'm right sorry about that, ma'am. I'm Mayor Withers, and I was the one who hired you. We weren't expecting you until next week for the grand ribbon-cutting ceremony. There was going to be music and dancing... Something the town would remember." He looked up to the burned-out building and slowly shook his head. "It's a real shame. Hank Henley, a miner who struck it rich, died and left his money to the town for this library. Had drawings and everything set aside at his lawyers for when he passed. It was almost done. The books arrived last week and were inside, too."

Following his gaze, she felt fresh tears rush to her eyes. Her only thought—it's all gone. "The books, too? Nothing salvageable?" She glanced from one man to the other.

"Sorry, Ma'am. The fire was well impossible to control by the time I got here. I think the workmen left linseed oil and stain that contributed to the conflagration. It was hot as he…well, it was real hot there for a while." The young man seemed to appear sheepish beneath the smeared grime, but it was difficult for her to tell.

"Will the town rebuild? I mean, perhaps I can get another job until it's ready to open." She hoped she didn't sound as desperate as she was beginning to feel.

The mayor responded, "I'm sorry, Miss Lorelei, I'm afraid not. We couldn't afford this one. Like I said, it was a bequeath from Hank. It was a great deal of money and the town was going to cover your salary when taxes were paid. We don't have it to give you now, and if there ain't a library, we don't have a need for a librarian."

"Yes, I understand budgets and such, Mayor. Is there any work in town for a female?"

He looked down at his shoes and then to the young man's shoes. "The bank just hired a new teller, but Jason would never have hired a woman anyways. No, ma'am, I can't think of a place for you to work at all.

4

We got a teacher, nice young man out of Omaha. Should be able to keep the boys at school in line. Knows he's allowed to whip 'em if he needs."

She noticed the younger man who had remained with them stood a little taller as the mayor spoke. Just then, the mayor looked across the street and yelled.

"Walt, hey, Walt, I need to talk to you." He ambled off, his words and heavy breathing mingling so she couldn't tell one from the other.

"Ma'am, my name's Luke Foster, and I have a place 'bout an hour out of town. Just a small ranch with me and my younger brothers. I can't pay much, but I need a housekeeper who can cook and such. It isn't fancy like being a librarian, and as I said, I can't pay much, but it will be a roof over your head and food in your belly."

Overwhelmed with the generosity of this stranger, she faltered. "I, I appreciate the offer, but I should find another position. I need to stay in town to do that."

"Yes, Ma'am, but I know this town pretty well, and there ain't been any jobs for a woman here in a few years. What women work here are wives of the business owners or ones that work over the saloon."

She must have made a squeak or gasp since his face under the smudge was definitely redder. She could see it on his neck too where the collar of the shirt opened.

"I didn't mean you should try there or anything, I was just trying to warn you off…"

Lorelei tried to sound prim and proper as any librarian ever had. "I understand your concern. Most librarians are men, also, so I understand the problems I face. All women do, yet we keep making strides in the workplace."

"Yes, Ma'am, I didn't mean nothin' by it. My mama would whip me if she thought I'd been disrespectful to a lady. But what are you planning? I hate to leave you standing here in the street like this."

The mayor came huffing back. "Have you made any plans, Miss Sanders? The hotel is right down the street, and it has a good restaurant I can recommend."

Just then, her stomach rumbled in protest of hearing about food knowing she had nothing left to buy any with.

"I was just offering Miss Sanders a housekeeping job out to my ranch, but…"

The mayor interrupted with a scold, "Luke, what are you thinking of asking a fine upstanding woman like this to live out at that ranch with you and your wild brothers. What would people say? What kind of a woman would accept a position like that? Not a lady, that's for sure."

Luke shot back only louder, "What do you mean by that? My brothers have all been raised as gentlemen. We would no more be discourteous to a lady than to eat our own socks. Why would you even say such a thing as that?"

"Wasn't that one of your brothers who run Miss Emmy's bloomers up the flagpole at school? He's the reason we only hire male teachers now. Poor old lady couldn't go to church on Sunday she was so mortified."

"It's not like they were dirty or anything. He stole them off her clothesline, so he didn't see a whole lot of difference between her letting them blow in the breeze or him letting them blow in the breeze. He was only teasing, and it was done on a dare."

"From one of your other brothers. They keep one another going, Luke. You've lost control of them, and now they do whatever they want."

"I'm doin' my best. I can't be with them all the time. I have to work the ranch, cut hay, raise grains…I don't have time to babysit them. That's why I thought a housekeeper was a good idea."

"It is a good idea, but not for a proper young lady like Miss Sanders. They need discipline, and you fail to give it to them."

"That isn't fair. The teacher doesn't like them, so he says bad things about them. Anything that goes wrong or breaks around that school gets blamed on my bothers."

Lorelei tried not to let the argument happening practically in her lap distract her. She had few options and was thousands of miles from home. If a city where you have no ties, no family, and no hope was home.

She mentally tallied up the few coins in her reticule and came up with a disappointing amount. Not enough for a night in the hotel she was sure, let alone a meal. Her stomach grumbled loudly, and she slammed her hand across it to stop the noisy rumbling. Now that the chance of a meal had been introduced, her body was making its vote known as to how to spend her funds.

The argument next to her continued. The mayor said firmly, "You can't expect a respectable female to step on that ranch without a marriage certificate in her hand."

The cowboy retorted, "You make it sound as if that was an impossibility. I'll have you know there are several women in this town who would marry me."

"Oh yeah, then why aren't you married? Why

didn't you ask Miss Sanders since you're such a catch?" The argument seemed to escalate between the two men.

"I would have, but we don't know one another. I don't have time to woo a woman if I don't have time to run the ranch and raise my brothers. It's not like I haven't thought about one of those mail-order brides. Just takes time, which we have already decided I don't have enough of."

Lorelei thought about that for a minute. She knew about the advertisements offering women wedding rings to come west and marry men they had never seen, never spoke to, before saying "I do." She tried to decide how she felt about that. She wasn't sure she could marry a complete stranger, a man who she knew nothing about. And what if he looked like the mayor? They probably all did. Would a handsome man need to advertise for a wife, or would women find him? Gravitate to him.

She couldn't think of any way to get herself out of this mess. Her money was in short supply, she had no friends or family to rely upon, she was in a town far from any others so options were limited, and her damn stomach would not stop rumbling!

"I'll do it! I'll marry him and take care of his house and young brothers. I can do it, I can marry him," she blurted out over the men's raised voices that came to an abrupt stop.

The mayor's brows rose, and a smile came across his still soot-covered face. "Why I think that's a fine idea, Miss Sanders. I know it will take a load of worry off my mind. I wasn't sure how you would get on, and now I needn't feel guilty about the job disappearing up in smoke."

"W-wait a minute. I mean, I know I offered Miss Sanders a job and all, but I hadn't planned on getting a wife." The rancher seemed flummoxed.

The mayor stared hard at the younger man. "Did you intend to take her out there to that bachelor household and ruin her reputation? Ruin her so any decent man would turn away from her? Would never make her an honorable offer of marriage?"

"Not if you put it like that, Mayor. I just meant for her to stay awhile until things were tidy and she had some travelling money."

Lorelei felt fresh tears fill her eyes and she sniffed to cover the sound of her stomach. "I understand. It sounds as if, ah, Luke has other plans than marriage. I understand. I do."

"Ma'am, it's not that I find anything about you less than perfect, but I came into town for fence posts and my brothers won't understand how I came to bring back a wife."

By now, she was feeling a complete fool for saying she would wed him. He hadn't actually asked her. She was thinking that of the two of them she would prefer the younger, taller man rather than the wheezing, rotund one. Her desperation had gotten the better of her, and now she would have to figure something else out.

She heard the words hissed out on a long breath. "I'll do it. I'll marry her if you, Mayor, stop looking at me like I'm depraved and, Ma'am, if you'll quit cryin'."

Relief almost overwhelmed her. She had a roof over her head and someone who would make sure she had food. She would have a home to depend on. Wiping her eyes again, she hoped she didn't appear as bad as the men in front of her did. They both looked like some sort of raccoon with light eyes and dark face. At least Luke made a cute raccoon with dimples that showed with the slightest smile.

"Walt! Bring Charlie over here for a minute," the mayor called over to the men still working on the hand-pumper.

She glanced around and saw Luke do the same with a wary expression as he looked between the men and the mayor. "Ah, Mayor, what's your plan here?"

"Why as mayor I can marry you right here and now. No need getting the reverend involved now is there? You don't want everyone knowin' your business."

Luke looked around again as if he was searching for an escape. "But ain't it a little soon? I mean, can't we wait for a day or two?"

The mayor looked at her and pointed. "What do you think this little lady is gonna do tonight while you git yourself ready to be a man? If I'm not mistaken, she hasn't much money and no way to get any. If she did, she wouldn't have accepted your proposal."

Her intended glanced over to meet her gaze and firmed his lips. "But we hardly know one another. I thought you meant marriage later, after a while."

The mayor became belligerent. "When Luke? Once you take her home to the ranch, her reputation will be in shreds. She wouldn't be able to come to town and hold her head up."

Lorelei felt as if her impulsiveness might have forced this kind young man into offering for her, and she knew that crying wasn't fair either, although the tears weren't contrived. She was tired and depressed seeing her planned life literally go up in smoke. Desperation forced her to make a quick decision—a leap of faith in the fullest meaning of the term.

"I think Mister, ah, Luke is right. We don't know one another, and perhaps I was too precipitous because I am emotional over seeing the library like this." She waved her hand toward the smoking rubble and felt the tears begin again.

And she didn't want to cry again. She really didn't want to put any pressure on Luke. And unexpectedly, her stomach rumbled, and she could not believe her humiliation since the man who was called, Walt, and his fellow firefighter, Charlie, arrived in answer to the mayor's request.

She had to stop this. "Gentlemen, thank you for coming over, but I've changed my mind. So sorry to bother you after your hard work this morning."

"No, Lorelei, we can do this today. It will be best for everyone. I can see that now. Mayor, whenever you're ready." Luke faced her and smiled encouragingly or at least she took it for a smile. It came out more as a grimace, but she knew she had no other option, no other way to support herself.

Closing her eyes, she made a silent prayer before nodding. She was becoming some man's bride in an ash-covered pelisse in front of grimed-faced strangers.

The mayor cleared his voice and began the ceremony. Lorelei hoped her voice would work when it came her time to say her vows. Her vocal cords tightened, and her mouth went dry. The taste of the fire was the only thing she concentrated on fearing she would run if she thought about anything else.

The mayor said her name, bringing her attention to him and the words. With some coaching, she parroted the words, "I do" before relief filled her at being left to think again. She noticed a piece of ash floating down lazily landing on her nose so that she blew it away with a short, sharp breath through her lips.

Thinking was what she should not be doing. Thinking would make her denounce the whole plan. Thinking would have her climbing back onto the train without a ticket. Thinking is what got her to this point in her life. The point where she put faith in a stranger and locked her life with his because he had kind eyes and dimples. Thinking is what got her to stand in one place long enough to hear the mayor pronounce them man and wife.

The two witnesses wandered back to the piece of machinery sitting idly in the center of the street. The mayor beamed at them saying, "Both of you follow me back to my office, and we'll finish with the signatures."

Feeling as if she were in a giant bubble, she walked along behind the two men who were in quiet conversation. They turned into a door marked with gold leaf paint announcing it as the office of legal counsel Amos Withers, Esquire and Judge Wm Withers. "My son is gone, so wait a moment for me to get the license filled out. Then a signature is all we need, oh, and the marriage fee of course."

Luke gave the older man an unreadable expression but reached two fingers into his front pocket searching for coins and placed some on the desk in front of him.

Signing her name for the last time, the enormity of what she had just done hit Lorelei in her still empty stomach. She placed her hand onto the desk to steady herself while Luke, her husband, accepted a copy of the marriage certificate.

He nodded as he passed her, and she gathered her skirts and hurried behind trying to keep up with his long strides eating up the boardwalk. He stopped at a wagon tied to the hitching post outside the Seed and Feed Store.

"You got bags at the station?"

She realized he was speaking to her and startled. "Yes, I left them when I saw all the smoke down the street and went to see if I could help."

"Same with me, although I got here as the flames burst through the roof. Do you need help up?" He nodded toward the wagon, and she scurried up the two steps and onto the bench seat realizing how sooty her skirts were.

CHAPTER TWO

Luke kept thinking of questions he would like answers to, but then kept silent rethinking how it would sound coming from him. Would she think him curious or rude? Would she answer him, but resent him asking? And did any questions matter since they were already married?

He went over what he would tell his brothers, especially Matt who was only a year younger and second in command. They usually consulted with one another before either of them made any decisions that would affect the ranch and family. Matt would have much to say about this breach.

He didn't dare look at the young woman next to him. He'd been attracted to her right from the first sight of her standing there crying in the street. He had never had a reaction similar to the draw this woman had on him. Usually, he stayed away from women. He didn't have the time, he didn't have the money, and he didn't have the inclination.

Not that he didn't like women. He liked them real well, but he made do with the short visits to ones who lived above saloons and made their trade known. He wasn't ready for a commitment. And now look at him. A married man taking his bride home and worried as hell his brothers would spook her away.

He almost felt like laughing. He was worried his

brothers would scare away the wife he never meant to get at a time he wasn't ready. Maybe it would be best if she took one look at the ranch and the work she would be expected to keep up with and go runnin' for the hills. It would serve him right for foolishly marrying her and for the mayor to foist his librarian onto him.

He snuck a quick glance her way. She was pretty even under the grit and grime. He probably looked no better, so why had she accepted the proposal? Well, not exactly a proposal, but she seemed keen on the idea of going out to the ranch as a housekeeper. Her hair was tidy and blond. Her eyes, he remembered gazing into them and thinking of a fawn he saw once. Soft, brown eyes, almond shaped with long dark lashes. He didn't have the guts to kill anything after looking into that young doe's eyes that morning. His stomach kind of felt that same way now.

He tried not to think about how he felt. It would make it that much more difficult when he introduced her to his brothers. Matt in particular would give him grief over his new bride. Especially if he remembered the conversation of just a few weeks ago.

The two of them had been discussing the needs of the ranch and where the money would come from to do everything. Matt wanted to add some specialty wood to the budget, and Luke didn't see the need for it. There were plenty of trees on the ranch Matt could use for his projects. After all, they didn't benefit from his hobby although each of the boys had a piece of furniture Matt made for them.

Now he had to explain how the cost of a wife fit in with the budget. How the ranch could afford a whole new person. He hoped Matt waited until she was out of earshot before the heckling and questions began. This was definitely a pickle, and he didn't want to have his new wife upset.

His wife. How in the hell had he gotten talked into this? He knew the mayor was upset about the fire. The man had bemoaned the loss of the library and all the books all through the time they fought the blaze. Luke moved twice so he didn't have to hear about the cost of this or that as it burned. Then the lamenting of how to inform the new librarian who was coming all the way from Ohio that there was no library or job.

He never mentioned the fact she was a beautiful young woman who didn't have any other means of support. Or that he would see her outside the library and be drawn to her, which was completely at odds with his usual behavior. He wasn't a flirt like his brother, Matt, or romantic like his brother, Bart. Luke hadn't thought of a wife although he thought he would be married at some point. Once the ranch was prosperous and he had time to devote to finding a woman he wanted to live with for the rest of his life.

If he thought about what that woman would be like, she might have been a lot like the woman sitting quietly next to him. Now he would never know, he never needed to know. He had the wife and all he had to do was live the rest of his life with her.

Turning off the main road, he guided the team onto the two-track leading through the gate marking it the Lucky Seven. The name chosen by his father a year before he died falling off the barn roof breaking his back and leaving the ranch and family in Luke's sixteen-year-old hands.

Luke shook his head. He didn't want to think about

those times. The fear he would let his family, his grieving mother, down in any way drove him to desperation. He worked double time, not coming in until exhaustion drove him to his bed, falling onto the rumpled sheets fully dressed.

That was while his mother still lived. They lost her less than two years later and by then the rest of the family looked to him for guidance and strength. He was their guardian and took his obligations to heart. His life could wait until theirs was secured. Now he had another who depended on him. As he saw the rooftops come into view, he clicked his tongue to the horses, and they sped up seeking the comfort of their stalls and food.

Feeling the woman next to him sit up straighter, she must have realized this was their destination, her home. He didn't know what to say, how to welcome her, while at the same time how to explain to his brothers. He couldn't exactly say he had been coerced into marriage by the mayor or by feelings of pity. This wasn't going to be easy, but it could mean the difference between her staying or asking to be taken back to town.

The wagon pulled up in front of a single-story wooden structure connecting two flanking two-storied structures. The man beside her, no, she had to start thinking of him as her husband, pulled the brake before wrapping the reins around it and jumping down. She heard him drop the wagon's gate and pull her trunk towards him.

Looking up at the house again, she took in the number of windows across the upper stories and at least two of them were wide open on each side. The covered porch across the front of the single-story portion looked inviting with a swing and several chairs, but it needed sweeping. She was about to dismount when she saw a tall man, taller than her husband, stride out of the barn, remove his leather gloves, and slap them against his thigh causing small puffs of dust to fly into the hot, dry air.

She watched as his familiar, sparkling blue eyes looked her over thoroughly. His smile was intriguing, and she sat in place watching him approach. She felt her lips curve in response to his friendly welcome.

"Luke, it took you long enough. I was beginning to worry you broke an axle or something, but I see you had good luck on your trip."

Her husband continued to wrestle her trunk to the porch before he stopped to say anything. She watched the other man look questioningly at his older brother taking in the soot-covered clothes and face then at her in the same condition.

"Luke? What happened?"

"Ah, I, ah. This is my wife, Lorelei Sanders, I mean, Foster. We got married this morning after the new library burned down."

"I'm not sure how those things are linked, but welcome to my new sister-in-law. I'm Matthew, by the way." He went to her side and put out his hand to help her dismount. "Anyone hurt? In the fire, I mean."

She gathered her skirts and found the step with her half-boot before accepting his bare hand with her gloved one. "Thank you."

Luke strode back to the rear of the wagon to retrieve her hand luggage. "No!"

Matthew's brows rose at the sharp answer but

continued to help her up the three porch steps before allowing her to take her hand back. Almost as if these two men had different mothers. Perhaps they had. She knew nothing about her husband or the family he brought her into. She stood not knowing what else to do and waited as the men talked.

"I'll take the wagon, Luke, while you show your wife around. She might like to use the facilities and then maybe a bath and get cleaned up. I'll keep the others away from the house for a couple of hours. Take her trunk to your room so she has her things. Then she can rest or look around the house."

She saw the hard expression pass between the brothers and wanted to be anywhere but there. Being stranded in a western town without any funds was beginning to seem the lesser of two evils.

"I know how to take care of a wife," Luke growled at his brother.

"It doesn't appear that way to me." Matthew climbed onto the bench and took the reins, snapping them against the hind ends of the team.

Luke brought the rest of her luggage, and she followed him through the doorway to a parlor. It was well furnished with the draperies pulled back to allow the light in. And although things could use a good dusting, it was better than she expected from a bachelor establishment. She had imagined it to be much worse on the ride from town. She had had over an hour to allow her fears and imagination to run wild.

Along with an upholstered sofa, there were two chairs and several tables. A lovely wooden shelf held a carved hummingbird in flight and a lifelike prairie dog. Each looked as if done by the same artist.

She followed her husband up the stairs but had a glimpse of the kitchen through an open doorway on the opposite side of the room. She went up the narrow steps into an open area before entering through a doorway to another room. This was a bedroom with a single, wide bed and a washstand with shaving gear on top.

A man's room then. Her husband's room and now hers. She felt herself begin to sweat and wanted to remove her coat so badly. But would that send the wrong message to the man making room next to her valise for her trunk before he brought it up?

"The privy's out the back door, and I'll pull down the tub from the laundry room wall just off the kitchen. There's water in the tank on the reservoir on the stove. Should be a towel there, too."

"I'm sure I can manage. What about you?" He snapped his head up to look at her. "I mean, will you be taking a bath, too? Should I, ah, dump the water and heat more for you?" Thinking of them sharing bath water was too intimate for her to say aloud. She thought he might be blushing again in which she took comfort. As if such ideas were embarrassing and foreign to him as well.

"No, in the summer, we use a large holding tank out behind the barn. It's always cool, and the horses don't seem to mind."

She nodded as if she understood how such a thing could replace a warm bath with plenty of soap.

He left as she pulled a clean dress and underclothes from the case making them into a bundle so no lacy bits showed. The last thing she grabbed was the brush before Luke came in carrying the bulky trunk.

The house was eerily quiet. She stopped abruptly

when one of the steps creaked as she tread on it. Smiling at her own timidity, she took the rest of the stairs as if she had been walking down these steps and through this house her whole life. She didn't waste time looking over her new domain, but instead marched to the room off the kitchen and found herself on an enclosed porch. Signs of other inhabitants surrounded the tub placed at one end of the small room.

There was an empty wooden bucket with a wood and rope handle beside the tub. She set her clothing on a chair near some boots before going back into the kitchen and the big black stove she saw there. It took several trips, but the reservoir still had warm water in it and the tub was full along with a bucketful set aside to rinse her hair.

There was soap and a clean towel as Luke said so she nervously undressed keeping an eye on the door to the backyard, which she had already been through to use the privy. Removing her last vestige of clothing was difficult, and she sank quickly into the water, taking comfort in the fact the water covered most of her nakedness.

She didn't waste time enjoying the soothing heat or fragrant soap but rubbed what suds she could manage out of the bar of soap and washed her hair. Taking a metal ladle, she poured clean water over her head allowing it to run down her back. There seemed to be a fine film of soot floating, making rainbows in the soap bubbles.

The rest of her ablutions were completed, and she hesitated to stand and feel exposed in this new environment. Looking around and listening, she finally took the chance to stand, dry off, and redress, including the corset so she was completely, reputably garbed.

Exhaling a deep breath, she unwrapped her hair so she could brush it out. She normally wouldn't do this fully clothed, but most of the water had soaked into the towel and the rest would dry as the day went on. She braided the mass while fine strands sprung up freely around her nape and ears. Then using a couple of hairpins, she coiled it at the back of her neck.

Shaking her clothing vigorously outside dislodged most of the ash. She would have to take more time with her hat later. The feather was the only part looking as if it hadn't been worn in the Chicago fire. It wasn't as if more than her head bore the brunt of the fire's aftermath. She had been traveling for days by train, and some of the other travelers insisted on riding with the windows open. Throughout the train car, small holes scarred the seats, and burn marks littered the wood floor caused by cinders and embers coming from the large stacks on top of the engine.

But that was all behind her now. From now on, this would be her home, and she would be happy and content here. She hung up the wet towel and began emptying the water using the bucket. She poured it over the neglected kitchen garden, although it appeared there were volunteer vegetables and some herbs still struggling to survive. She recognized garlic and sage as well as dill and rosemary. Every time she came out with another bucket, she spotted more and more plants she recognized. In the back against the house, there were tomatoes as well as summer squash.

Seeing the plants, she realized her husband and his brothers would be expecting a meal, and since she was the woman of the house, it was up to her to provide it.

She hoped there was more in the pantry than what was in the garden. A church mouse would starve on this puny amount. Her stomach began its chorus of growls now she was thinking of food again.

Her father hadn't raised a quitter, so she turned the tub on end leaning against the wall and returned the bucket to its hook next to it. The kitchen was neat, and things seemed to be in place. Several pots and pans hung on the back wall by the stove with a cupboard nearby having an enamel top she could pull out to work on. Opposite that was the sink and red hand pump. She didn't see a pantry, so what food there was must be in the cupboard and hutch in the dining room to the front of the house.

It wasn't a formal dining room like she and her father had in Ohio. This one was more utilitarian. A long, scarred table with several chairs around it sat in the center of the room on the polished floorboards. The handsome breakfront was closest to the kitchen with dishes and cups showing through the glass doors. She pulled open one drawer to find flatware and knives. Other kitchen utensils took up the second drawer, and she remembered seeing a jar of them on the warming shelf of the stove.

The double doors on the bottom of the hutch opened from the center, and she stared at several sacks of dried white beans advertising they came all the way from Michigan, one of her previously neighboring states. Besides coffee, that was all there was. She felt disappointed until she realized there was still the cabinet, and she went hopefully back to the kitchen.

Some luck there. A couple of pounds of flour in the metal bin and sack of cornmeal. Finding a quart of canned peaches made her heart actually beat faster. She jumped when she heard a young voice behind her.

"Are you really my sister-in-law?"

She turned, laughing at her nervous reaction to find a boy of about nine with those same blue eyes as his brothers, only having lighter hair, almost straw-colored. "I am if you're one of Luke's brothers."

"I'm Simon and the youngest. Ma was naming us after the disciples but didn't get through all twelve. I don't remember her, but Matt says she was a real nice ma."

"I'm sure she was. I'm sorry you never got to know her." She wasn't sure what else to say to the boy who stood there in denim bib overalls a little too big for him, the hems worn off from dragging across floorboards.

"I brought in the eggs for you. We usually have beans for supper, but I don't see any soaking."

She glanced toward the stove. "I didn't see any either. What else would you eat if you didn't have beans?"

"Eggs or biscuits. Ham sometimes or chicken when Matt feels like frying it up."

Her mind leaped at that knowledge. "I heard roosters. Do you think I could kill one for dinner?"

"You're gonna cook? I can kill the chickens if'n you're gonna fry 'em."

"I'll put the water on to boil then and see to finding lard and anything else for supper."

She went back to the cupboard with new eyes and found several things to make a meal with, including those dried beans for breakfast.

CHAPTER THREE

Lorelei looked at the table set with white and flowered plates, nickel-plated flatware, and metal coffee cups. She debated with herself about adding the glass of flowers she picked in the garden when she gathered the sage and garlic.

Simon came in sniffing the air, his face shiny with a fresh washing. She noticed he left his boots in the back porch so the house floors stayed cleaner. She thought the boy well-behaved. He had even plucked the chickens before bringing them in to be cooked.

"Everything is ready and waiting in the oven to stay warm. I hope Luke and Matt get back soon. I'm afraid I'm rather hungry myself."

"They would have been in here if they knew what you made. I've never ate a meal that smells as good as yours does."

"Just fried chicken and giblet gravy with biscuits. I fried green tomatoes and summer squash, but there weren't any potatoes. I love mashed potatoes with chicken gravy, but at this point, any food would be ambrosia."

"What's ambro...ambros...ia?"

Just as she was trying to explain, she heard a loud clang of a bell and realized it was the one nailed to the side of the back door. She turned expectantly toward the door and brushed down the apron she wore over her skirt. Feeling nervous, she felt a smile waver on her face.

Luke was the first one through the door, his nose leading him to look over at the stove with a smile. "You cooked? I was expecting to fry up some eggs and maybe biscuits if there was enough flour."

Matthew came in next, his eyes flashing with amusement. "I knew she was more than a pretty face. What's for supper, Sis?"

She couldn't stop the full-blown smile that pushed its way through her nervousness. Then felt it turn to concern as she saw another full-grown man enter and knew he was a brother since he had the same blue eyes, and then another and another and another. My goodness, it was like an army of Fosters in various stages of growth. All going to be tall, blue-eyed handsome devils. They each had a dimpled smile and cleft in their chin.

The older young men were dressed as Luke and Matthew with long-sleeve shirts, trousers, and socks or bare feet. The twins had on bib overalls and shirts much like Simon's, which is where his probably came from as the twins outgrew them.

Her mind went to the sixteen pieces of fried chicken and two dozen biscuits keeping warm in the oven, thinking it should be enough. She thought she had been making enough for lunch tomorrow, but she would need to make something more in the morning.

"Lorelei, you met Matt, and I see you know Simon. These are my other brothers by descending age— Bartholomew, Andrew, and twins Peter and Paul. Boys, smells like time to eat."

She waved them to the table saying, "I only set for

four. I'm afraid I wasn't aware of all the members in Luke's family. But I made enough for an army. And an army is what I have." She laughed, taking a dish towel to pull the pot and platters from the oven as one of the twins set more plates and flatware out.

Lorelei set everything on the table with Matt helping carry the heavier tray and setting them in front of the family who sat waiting politely until she sat down. Matt held her chair for her at the foot of the table before taking a seat to her right.

She bowed her head and said a silent grace. When she raised it, everyone was looking at her with various expressions on their faces. She smiled taking a biscuit and passed the basket to her left. That set off an explosion of motion as each one served themselves pieces of chicken and biscuits with ladle or fork. In less time than she would have thought plates were filled, mouths were full and quiet reigned.

There were many sounds of contentment, not any less than her own as she finished the two biscuits with giblet gravy and the thigh that was her favorite piece of chicken. She stood taking her empty plate with her and returned with a peach torte, the crust toasty brown. She cut the pie in eight even pieces, placing one on each plate as Matthew passed them around the table. Most of the plates were empty by the time the last one was set in front of her.

The obvious success of her meal gave her a sense of self-confidence as she took the first forkful of dessert. She glanced up to see her new family looking longingly at the now empty platter and gravy pot. She had seen either Peter or Paul wipe the bottom of the gravy pan with the last of the biscuits.

But these young men were still hungry. She didn't need to be raised with boys to know the look of yearning as they thanked her politely and began to leave the table.

She stood, annoyed with herself for being so slow to realize the difference between someone being pleased with the meal and being content. "Sit back down all of you. I must apologize that I forgot I was not simply cooking for six boys, but I was cooking for six hardworking boys. I'll have a batch of flapjacks mixed up in a minute. Anyone know if you have molasses or syrup?"

Simon jumped up and ran to the cupboard bringing back a crock of honey and a mason jar of molasses. "We run out of syrup for the year. Gotta wait till next spring."

She sent out the first batch of flapjacks and the men around the table became quiet once again. Eventually, Matthew came over to stand by her side.

"We're finally filling up these boys' hollow legs." He glanced over his shoulder toward the table. "You know your supper was the best we've had in years. I'm afraid none of us are very good in the kitchen, and we've let things deteriorate. I'm amazed you found that much food."

"I didn't know there were so many of you. I mean, Luke and I didn't discuss his family other than he was the eldest. When I met you and Simon, I thought I had met all of them. I never asked."

"You shouldn't have had to ask. I don't know what happened this morning, but you deserve to be treated better."

"I'm fine, Matthew. Luke came to my rescue, and I

sincerely appreciate his help."

The clatter of dishes made them both startle toward the sink as Luke picked up the handle on the pump and began splashing water over the scraped-clean plates.

"No, Luke, I'll do those. Both of you go and rest. You've had a big day already, and I planned to do these up. It won't take that long." She saw the twins look at one another smiling as they brought the last of the dishes into the kitchen.

She put the last of the cook pans on the still-hot stove to dry. Checking on the beans soaking in a kettle on the counter before hanging up the wet dish towels, she hesitated to go into the parlor where she heard voices. But she had to go through that room to reach the stairs to her room, so she pasted on a smile and strode into the pleasantly warm parlor.

Luke jumped up as soon as he saw his wife enter the room. She was rosy-faced from washing the dishes over the steamy water. He gave a hard look to Matt who took the hint.

"I'm for my bed." Matt stretched and yawned, and Luke thought it appeared rather contrived, although Lorelei didn't seem to notice.

"Goodnight, Matthew. Thank you for your help," she said standing unsure in the archway.

"Anytime. I'll see you both in the morning." Matthew whistled as he climbed the set of stairs to the rooms over the dining room and kitchen.

Luke had sat on the far end of the sofa so he could watch her finish her work. Intrigued by the sway of her fanny as she washed and stacked, he waited for her to join him. She appeared wary as he patted the sofa beside him. "We need to talk."

Lorelei nodded and sat gingerly on the edge of his mother's favorite piece of furniture. Pulling her into his side, he placed his arm over her shoulder.

"I wanted you to know I was impressed with the meal you provided for me and my brothers. I meant to return after I got cleaned up but got called out to see to a late birth. The calf was breech, and no one saw the problem for several hours."

She seemed accepting of his arm along the back of the sofa which he felt was a good sign, although she was sitting stiffly. Probably not used to being around men. Well, there's a lot of men in this house so...

"Did you save them?" she asked hesitantly, as if afraid to hear about the animals coming to harm.

"Yes, but neither will thank me for it. Probably painful for both, and my foot got stepped on more than once."

"I didn't expect you to change your day for me. After all, it wasn't as if we planned this."

He thought she sounded contrite. "I know. When I realized you didn't even know how many brothers I had... I realized I hadn't paid as much attention to you as I should have done."

"Luke, you mustn't worry about me. Concentrate on your ranch and family as usual. I appreciate the chance you have given me. I don't know where I would be right now if you hadn't accepted the mayor's suggestion."

"Mayor Withers is a man to be reckoned with, a man who seems to get his own way most times." He shook his head remembering how quickly he found himself married.

"Are you regretting it? I mean, now he can't push

you into doing something you don't want to do."

He glanced over and caught the expression of fear and desperation on her face.

"It only helped me make a decision I should have made long ago. But as the mayor said, there aren't many young women in town. The boys have need of a female's view of things. They have lived in this all-male household for too long. The twins don't remember much about Ma and nothing of Pa. I feel pressure to be both mother and father, and I don't feel up to it. I didn't realize how much it weighed on me until I came home to find the house filled with the smells of a homemade dinner. It was, I don't know…overwhelming, I guess. And you did it all alone."

"Simon was a big help, but we need to do something about the food situation. There isn't enough here if the boys eat like they did this evening."

"They always seem hungry. I was embarrassed at how much they put away tonight, but I wasn't much better. I guess beans aren't as stimulating to a young boy's appetite."

"The younger boys need milk, not coffee. They're still growing. Among all those cattle, do you have a cow out there you can milk?"

"I guess—once she gets used to the indignity of it." He chuckled thinking about a field heifer placidly allowing itself to be milked.

"There is enough cornmeal for a couple more meals I think, but then…"

"Don't worry about it. I'll take you into town in the morning, and we'll stock up with anything you think we need. It isn't the money as much as taking time out to shop, and as I said, none of us can cook very well.

Beans and fried meats are about it. Can't make bread, although I burn a pretty good biscuit and, of course, corn bread." He listened to the short menu and wasn't impressed. "And coffee, can't forget about the coffee."

"I can see why the chicken and gravy went over so well then. I'll see how many chickens can be spared for the dinner table."

He stood and held his hand down to help her up. As she took it, he whispered, "Just don't give the chickens a vote." As Lorelei approached the open area at the top of the stairs, her feet faltered, and she stepped slower. About to place his hands on each side of her hips to steady her, he thought better of it. He wanted to reassure her that he didn't plan on this evening being the beginning of their married life.

It was a subject he thought they would have covered already, but he found the words hadn't come as easily as the plan. His plan was to wait until they knew one another, knew they could trust. Marriage was based on trust, and they were still strangers. But this was one conversation that was coming up sooner rather than later, and he had to face it head-on. When they both stood at the top of the stairs, he thought it time.

"Um, Lorelei, I mean to sleep in the baby room."

"The what?" She sounded startled.

"Here—this room at the top of the stairs while you take the bed in there. It was my folks' room, and the young 'uns slept out here so they could be heard from anywhere in the house if they cried. My folks kept their privacy to add to the family."

He saw her eyes get large, and he added, "Too soon for private family jokes, I guess. My folks didn't hide their love for one another. Of course, having baby right after baby so quickly kind of proved their point."

"I wasn't shocked. I was surprised you seem so open about it. Most people cringe even contemplating their parents, ah, doing that, um, being intimate."

"Just part of ranch life." He went past her to grab a pillow off the bed and the comforter from the foot of it before stepping out of the bedroom. "I'll leave my things in there if you don't mind. I'll ask permission to enter if I need something while you're in there."

He spread the quilt on the floor while she watched.

She still appeared concerned. "This isn't going to be very comfortable for you, Luke. Why don't I take the floor and you use the bed? That way you'll get a good night's sleep."

He glanced back at her now standing in the doorway. "No way is my wife sleeping on the floor if there is a bed available. I'll figure out a mattress tomorrow. There's a candle and matches next to the bed if you need to get up in the night. If there's nothing else you want, then I'll see you in the mornin'."

He saw her nod and close the door. He stood for a moment wondering if he could have made that go smoother but decided it was what it was and at least neither of them was in tears. He tossed the pillow into place and unbuttoned his shirt to pull it over his head. Stripping out of his trousers, he chided himself for not remembering to get the bottoms of his union suit to sleep in. If she did wake before him, she was going to see all his assets such as they are.

CHAPTER FOUR

She knew he was awake but didn't want to exit her room until he was gone. Unlike her father, she thought it unlikely Luke wore a nightshirt. She didn't want to run into a naked man first thing in the morning—or at any time if she were honest. She didn't even want to think about one. Even one as handsome as her husband.

A tap on her door made her jump as if the person on the other side would be able to discern her thoughts.

"Lorelei, may I come in and get a clean shirt? Well, cleaner than the one from yesterday."

"Certainly. I'm dressed and ready to go down and start breakfast."

She noted he was wearing socks and his trousers, his hair a little mussed from sleep. She turned away from his bare chest and pretended to wipe a wrinkle out of the sheets on the bed. "I'm amazed how neat things are in the house considering it's such a large family."

"One thing I did figure out early on is that if we were not to live like heathens, we would have to be practical. Everyone makes their bed each morning no matter what. If they pick it up, they put it away. On laundry day, which I confess is overdue, each one is responsible for taking their clothes off the line, folding them, and putting them away. We used to share making dinner and cleaning up afterward, but those duties pretty much fell to the twins."

Watching, he sniffed the undersleeve of the shirt in his hand before shrugging and pulling it over his head. She didn't know if she was amused or appalled. But she realized these men, these boys, were all doing more than they should to keep the ranch running. She concluded she could repay Luke for taking her in by making his life easier.

"I'll go on down to put the beans on. There's time for that, isn't there?" she asked, unsure how to go about being of help to him now that she faced the chance of doing so.

"Sure. I'm always the first one up."

She scrambled past him and hurried out through the kitchen. The call of nature came first, and then she would concentrate on breakfast.

Adding a big dollop of molasses to the drained beans, she placed them into the oven before stirring the coals and adding another couple of pieces of wood. Mixing up the corn bread, she used the last of the eggs and then ground the coffee beans to make coffee. Choosing the large pot, she remembered Luke's fondness for the drink.

Simon entered, his hair uncombed, while he struggled to hook the button into the bib overalls. "You're still here. It felt like a dream so I wuz 'fraid you weren't real."

"I'm still here, so you are either still dreaming, or I am real." She only meant to tease the boy, but he came to a stop and contemplated what she said.

"I guess that's possible. Do you think life could be one whole dream and then I'll wake up and have to live it all for real? Or maybe it's like do-overs. Like in a game. When you make the wrong chess move and you want the chance to do it over only Luke says you can't, but Matt always lets you?"

She absorbed the information to take out and think about later. Right now, she needed to get a breakfast ready. "I saw a comb out on the back porch yesterday next to the washstand. Why not finish getting ready and then help me set the table."

"You can pile the plates next to the stove and then everyone can help themselves when they get down. Some of us have work to do before breakfast so we eat after."

"That makes perfect sense to me. Thank you for the advice."

"I'll be back soon with the eggs. The chickens need to be let out and fed."

After the meal was cleared away, Lorelei came downstairs making sure her hat was secure to find her husband ready to take her to town.

"The wagon's already out back, and all I have to do is put on my boots."

She approved the habit of removing work boots before coming into the house. There was nothing worse than the smell of the barn inside a home, and sometimes it was impossible to get boots clean enough to walk across the carpet.

Luke was helping her onto the seat when Bart rode up, his horse lathered and breathing deeply. "Glad I caught you. We got a heifer stuck in a mud hole up past her belly. She's bawling something fierce, but I don't think she's hurt. Andy and I ain't strong enough to get her out, and we're afraid of breaking her leg trying."

Luke looked up at her apologetically. As she was about to tell him not to think anything about it and that she could work around the house instead, Matthew strode from the barn. His long legs ate up the ground quickly.

"What's all the commotion about?" Matt directed his question to Luke.

She could see Luke was undecided. "I'm needed to help get a stupid cow out of the mud." Peering up at her, he seemed apologetic. "I guess we'll have to postpone the shopping trip."

"I can go out and help the boys," Matt said but didn't seem surprised when Luke turned down the offer. "Then I can take my new sister-in-law to town and show her off. After all, we need that shopping done, or she won't have a chance to cook anything besides beans again. Even though they are the best beans I ever tasted." Then he actually winked at her!

She knew she blushed. What a thing to do and right in front of her husband, too. She thought it best for the men to decide what to do and who best to do it. At least Luke appeared regretful when he finally nodded to Matt.

He turned to her. "Get whatever you need. Matt will handle the sacks. We have accounts at all the stores, but the butcher actually owes us money. We get a hog from him every fall, but it's all but gone by summer. In exchange, we get him beef on the hoof." He looked around seeing Bart coming out of the barn with a saddled horse. "Sorry I couldn't go with you this time, but we'll get to talk after supper. I promise."

Matt came out of the back porch door, letting it slam shut on the spring, looking like he'd splashed water on his face and combed his hair. She made sure her skirts wouldn't touch his leg and waited facing forward.

"Relax, Sis, I've never lost a passenger yet. Of course, I'm usually on a horse alone…"

She had to laugh at his foolishness. "Are you ever serious?"

"I try not to be. Life's too short."

This time as she rode down the dirt track, she paid attention to what was around her. She wanted to know more about her husband and knowing his ranch was one of the best ways.

Matt's voice interrupted. "You know when Luke showed up yesterday, I was pleased he found someone to wed. Then I realized what that meant for me."

Lorelei never admitted to curiosity but knew she was overly so. "And that was what?"

"First, I was jealous, and then I felt a great weight lifted from my shoulders. I could move on and not feel as if I had let the boys down, let Luke down."

"Move on? You're leaving because I'm here? Don't do that. Don't feel that way. I would hate knowing I drove you from your home."

"You didn't. This is something I've wanted to do for ages but didn't want Luke to feel alone. It's hard to explain.

"Explain it to me, then it may be easier to explain to your brothers."

"When Pa died, I was jealous Ma thought Luke was the one who should take over. I was only a year younger and felt I knew it all as most fifteen-year-olds do. Anyway, I took orders as usual and things were going fine." He got quiet and gazed away as if trying to control his words and cope with his emotions. "Then Ma just gave up."

"What? What do you mean, 'gave up'?"

"She got smaller somehow and then sickly and then passed on. Simon wasn't much more than a baby and the twins about the age Simon is now. We all lost our way for a while. Bart and Andy quit school and refused to go back. They were always getting sent home anyways, and Luke and I didn't have the heart to fight them into returning.

"Simon went back to wetting the bed, so no one wanted to sleep with him. By then, we were all in the two bedrooms over the kitchen, Ma...Ma had stayed in the room you and Luke have now. No one took that room until about two years ago. Luke said it was foolish to leave a perfectly good bed empty when we were all crowded into the two rooms."

"It makes sense. Did that bother you, too? I mean, he seemed to be usurping the role of family leader."

"No, he took Simon with him, and I think once things calmed down, he stopped wetting the bed. He eventually came back over to the boy's side as we call it and fit right in again. We're a little like sardines in a can what with the beds lined up in rows, but we're used to it. Not much else we can do. The little ones aren't very little any longer."

"No, only Simon is going to change much now. Maybe the twins will get taller, fill out some."

"They will if you keep cooking as you do."

She took the compliment and looked around the main road they were now on. There were signs of other ranches, but they didn't pass anyone. "So, tell me where you would go if you decided to leave the family."

"Alaska." No hesitation. "Been dreaming about the place for years now. I'd go up there and carve me out a piece of the wilderness. Build something big so that people will remember I was there."

"A ranch?"

"No, ranching's fine work, and I don't mind it, but it isn't in my blood like it's in Luke's. He thinks about it every moment of every day. I know what needs to be done, but I do other things, too."

"Such as?" She knew she was leading him, but this was one way to learn about her new family, possibly about her own husband.

"My woodshop. It began with carving while I was out with the cattle, and then, I made a cradle when the twins were born since Ma only had the one. I fell in love with furniture making. I love the smell, the feel of rough wood, and then making it into something usable and decorative at the same time. I want to make a desk. You know the kind with lots of drawers and letter slots. But that takes too much time, so I settle with smaller less ornate pieces."

"Like the hutch? I noticed how lovely it was right off."

At his nod, another thought struck her. "Are there trees in Alaska? I've never read anything about it, but I think of it being snow and ice and polar bears."

"It has those things too and large untouched forests. I've been dreaming of going up there. Maybe I should go into logging or building furniture, maybe houses, maybe a whole town."

She chuckled. "I see the Fosters don't think small."

"No, when Pa came out to the territory, he bought enough land to raise double the cattle we do now. He must have had some idea he was going to have all these boys to keep busy."

They both rode quietly side by side before Matthew began his questions. "What about your Pa? Is he a farmer back in, where was it, Indiana?"

"No, he was a professor at Cincinnati College in Ohio. My mother died when I was very young, and he ended up taking me to work. It was said he kept me in a laundry basket until I began to crawl around. The women, none of whom were married, would take me from office to office during the day if he had classes. I was probably spoiled by all the attention."

"Did you miss not having a ma? I mean we older boys remember her well enough, but not the twins and certainly not Simon. It's like he blocked all that time right out of his mind. Never asks about her either."

"I didn't know any other life. After school each day, I went to my father's office and stayed with him until he left work. I got to love books as much as it seems you love woodworking."

"So, you became a librarian."

"Not quite as simple as that but, yes, I became a librarian. My father died recently, and although we had some savings, the medical costs took them all. So I was without a home or a job since I worked alongside my father. It seems the only reason I was working at all was because he insisted upon it, or he would have quit. Once he died, there was no reason to keep me on."

"Don't let people like that place a value on you and what you do. I bet you're a very good librarian, and Mayor Withers evidently saw your worth or he wouldn't have hired you."

She liked that this new brother-in-law would take

umbrage at how the university had treated her. It felt nice to know someone supported her abilities.

"I have a feeling I was hired because I was one of a few who would accept the salary the town was offering."

"Don't denigrate yourself. My sister-in-law is worth a lot more than anyone understands. And you're braver than anyone knows."

"How so?" She was laughing at his dramatic way of speaking, as if giving some kind of speech.

"You not only married a long-time bachelor, but the man has six brothers all in need of polishing to get the rough edges smoothed off."

"I didn't find you all that intimidating. I think a little blunting of the sharp points will be enough to start with."

She saw the town appear in the clearing ahead of them. Sitting straighter, she was glad she wore her best traveling dress and matching hat to face the curious eyes and inquisitive townsfolk. People she knew would have questions of the woman who arrived as a spinster librarian and left as a new bride.

Matthew pulled the wagon to a stop in front of the general store and helped her down the narrow steps. "I'll be back in a while, so take your time. You might keep in mind that I'm partial to berries. Any kind will do."

"I'll keep that in mind, Matthew, but berries are in season so I might not buy any. Maybe I'll find where they grow wild." She looked at the paper in her hand. "There is so much on the list I'm not sure where I'll put it all."

"If you didn't know, we have an ice cave built into

the hill by the house. There's still ice from winter so we can keep most meat in there."

"Thanks for letting me know. If there is a place things like potatoes and vegetables can be put, then I'll not hesitate to buy what we'll need for a couple of weeks."

Lorelei climbed the three steps to the boardwalk in front of the white clapboard store. Large windows on each side of the central door filled with a multitude of dishware and cooking items enticed her. Decorative hand-painted oil lamps stood beside high-buttoned shoes and ten-gallon hats. She pushed the wide door with the gold leaf lettering open and walked in.

The woman behind the counter raised her head from the ledger in front of her. "Hello, when you're ready to order just give a call. I'm Dorothy Johnston, and you must be Luke Foster's new bride."

"I am, and please call me Lorelei. I'm not used to being called anything else, yet."

"I understand. For weeks after I was married, if anyone called for Mrs. Johnston, I'd look around for my mother-in-law."

"I have a list here, but I would like to browse and see what else you have. Especially fresh vegetables or fruit."

As the woman read over the list, she said, "I think if we left it up to men, they would eat meat and bread, I swear. Luke and the boys ordered little besides beans and coffee. How they didn't get scurvy, I'll never know."

Lorelei was still smiling as she made her way to the notions department where she bought bobbins of thread and a packet of miscellaneous-sized buttons. She had noted the boys all were in need of having mending done.

Walking past the stacks of canned goods, she selected some she knew she could use. She kept devising meals as she found familiar items and spices. She checked on Dorothy, and the woman was climbing up and down ladders collecting the many items on the list.

Lorelei wandered toward the material and found some ready-made clothing as well.

As any good proprietress, Dorothy tried to enhance her sale as she called from across the store, "I have several catalogs of clothing if you care to look through them. I know those boys are probably growing like weeds, although I haven't seen them for months. Ever since they stopped attending school last spring."

"All of them left school? Even Simon?"

"Yes. There was some incident, and they left one day and never came back. The teacher isn't popular, but the school board hired him because he was considered tough enough to handle the older boys."

"Were they that bad, then?"

"Probably not, but I only have girls. My daughters said the boys spoke up and joked around, but weren't mean or dangerous. They certainly aren't afraid of the boys, so they must not have bullied any of the other students."

Lorelei had so much on her mind she was startled when Matthew appeared next to her. "If you ever want to know what's happening in Whitewater Rapids, this is the place to do so."

Smiling a welcome, she said, "I think I'm the main story right now. Several women have come in to look at me and then disappeared without buying anything."

He picked up a bar of facial soap and sniffed. "This is nice." He placed the bar under her nose, and she leaned toward him. She jumped when a sickly-sweet voice next to her spoke.

"Why Matt Foster, I thought this was your brother Luke's wife. Not trying to rustle her, are you? You two look pretty cozy." The woman speaking was made-up with dark outlines on her eyelids and her lips reddened. The gingham dress she wore had a low neckline and was too tight across the woman's breasts.

"I always wanted a sister. So much prettier than brothers, don't you think?" Matthew winked at Lorelei again, which made her giggle. She noticed Matthew hadn't reacted to the woman's presence, so had he known she was there?

The shorter woman appeared angry with Matthew but directed her words at Lorelei. "Tell Luke that Madeline said hello, won't you? Let him know I miss our little talks together."

Then she turned without saying anything to Matthew and sashayed out, her skirts swinging with each angry step as Lorelei watched. She lowered her eyes, thinking.

Matt stepped closer. "Look at me, Lorelei."

She raised her gaze from the soap in her hand to peer into the blue eyes so like her husband's. A husband who hadn't bothered to explain there was another woman who felt proprietary of him.

He took her hand in his rough one just like Luke's. "Listen to me. Luke never 'talked' with her. Never."

"How can you be so sure?" She hated sounding needy.

"Because I did. We never poach on one another's territory. It was a decision made years ago, when we both faced the facts, we may end up sleeping with the same woman. Neither of us found that acceptable. Now that both Bart and Andy are of an age to be going to town on their own it's going to become tricky. Thank God, Luke's out of the running."

She barked out a nervous laugh and quickly placed her gloved hand over her mouth peering around to see if anyone was close enough to hear. "Oh, Matthew, the things you say to me make me blush."

He grinned, the dimples showing through the heavy bristles on his face. "And I make you laugh. As long as I can, I'll make you laugh because I like the sound." His head turned to the counter. "Dorothy must have everything, let's add these to the pile and get home. I need to get the boards I bought hidden from Luke before he tears a strip off me."

CHAPTER FIVE

Lorelei changed into the oldest work dress she had and set the pig scalder on the firepit in the backyard. The water was boiling when she added the soap chips and shirts, pushing them under the water with a wood paddle after having prescrubbed them on the metal washboard. The socks were next, and she found many needing darning. She hoped there was yarn in the house somewhere or else they would need to wait for another trip to town.

She found a child's chamber pot filled with wooden clothespins and set up the mangle next to the rinse water. It started out as a daunting project, but once she decided to take it in batches, it seemed more manageable. She didn't want to invade the boys' rooms, so Matthew had brought their soiled clothes to her. She would have to figure out a system or maybe a basket on the porch. Something so she would know how much laundry was building up.

Each Foster came in that night with clean hands and faces and a pile of clean clothes. When they came in from work, each had taken their own clothes off the line and folded them. Just as Luke said they would.

"Thank you, Miss Lorelei. Yes, thank you. Thanks." They all worded their gratitude as they passed her and glanced expectantly at the stove.

"Supper is ready as soon as those clothes are

upstairs. I'll do the rest in the morning and start on the mending."

Luke stopped in front of her. "You don't have to do so much. Cooking is enough."

"Madeline says to say hello." She watched his eye for a flicker of movement, to see if she could tell if he lied.

His brows came down slightly as he cocked his head. "Who?"

"Never mind, I must have gotten the name wrong." Turning back to the stove, she continued, "Do you want to help me put the platters on? Tom, the butcher, gave me a nice big ham, so I baked it off with brown sugar and apples. They're from last fall so it was either bake them or make them into sauce."

"You don't have to worry about the boys. They're so glad to have someone else in charge of cooking they wouldn't complain about anything. But smelling this kitchen, I don't think I have to worry about this meal."

"I want you all to enjoy the meals. It's the least I can do for..."

Luke took her hand, his thumb rubbing over her palm. "I want to tell you now that you don't owe me anything. Never feel as if you are beholden to me or the others. We're happy you joined our family."

The thumping of bare feet on the steps reminded her to step away from him and take her chair. Luke did the same.

His brothers' eyes were all wide as they stared at the large platter of sliced ham alongside the green beans, biscuits, potato pancakes, slaw, and preserves. Pride filled Luke's heart having a wife as good at homemaking as he had. How else was he supposed to feel? She was perfect so far. And he was so undeserving. He had never done anything in his life to earn a woman like her. If he hadn't gone to town for those fence posts, he never would have fought that fire, and she might be married to some other lucky dog.

Simon nudged his arm so that he would take the bowl of steamed beans being passed around. He took some on his plate but kept wondering what he and Lorelei would talk about tonight. He promised himself they would get to know one another after the younger ones went to bed and the older ones made themselves scarce.

Matt even hinted maybe some time alone was due for the newly married couple. Even though the two of them argued the most, he could still depend on Matt as his second-in-command. The brother most responsible and able to care for the others and the ranch if anything should happen to Luke.

Lorelei accepted his brothers' praise and got up to refill bowls and coffee cups. She looked pink cheeked and pretty and lighthearted even though he knew she had worked a hard day, too. Shopping, laundry, cooking, and all without complaint. He had a saint— and it worried him.

What if she found it too much? What if she realized she could have it easier with a rancher just starting out or a single man in town. He couldn't think of one at the moment that wasn't old enough to be her father or so fresh-faced he wasn't shaving daily, yet. That information brought him some relief. He didn't seem to have much competition if she did plan to leave him. Although, there was the new teacher.

He realized he had eaten the whole meal without tasting much of it at all but knew it had been good. His brothers were taking their plates to the sink while his wife passed out baked apples, crisp skinned and fragrant of cinnamon from the oven.

After the meal was cleared, he stayed in the kitchen and helped wipe the dishes.

"Luke, I wish you would go sit and rest. These won't take me long."

"And they will take us even less time. Besides, I like having you alone."

She glanced into the parlor where Matt and Bart were reading and the twins played chess with Simon waiting in the wings to play the victor. She made no comment.

"This is about as alone as we're gonna get in this house. I may have misjudged how difficult it was going to be to woo my own wife." He brushed against her arm enjoying having her close even if they weren't actually by themselves.

"I thought we were just going to talk. I'm not sure I'm up to wooing." She seemed to be teasing with him, but he wondered if she wasn't just being shy.

"I know it's been a hard day for you. I told you not to try to do everything for the boys. They've been getting by so far."

She stopped washing dishes and looked up at him. "That reminds me. How long have the boys, the younger boys, been out of school? Do you know what caused them to be sent home?"

He wasn't expecting that. He didn't remember exactly. "Why do you ask? The twins are nearly sixteen and lots of boys quit at that age." He picked up another plate to dry.

"But Simon quit then, too."

"He did? I thought he was still going. He talks about his friend Toby all the time. Even brought him back here one afternoon."

"Was it a day they were both supposed to be in school?"

"I'm not sure." He was beginning to realize he may have stopped worrying about his brothers too soon.

She took the platter out of his hands. "You're going to wear the pattern right off that if you dry it any longer." Tipping the dishpan, his wife let the water go down the drain that emptied into the garden area.

She dimmed the lamp hanging from the wall hook. "I'm not saying Simon did anything wrong, but I think he's been avoiding school. Possibly getting this Toby to play hooky, too. But he's too young to quit, and I think the twins are, also. The jobs of the future are going to require more education than what they need to be ranchers. You don't expect all of the boys to stay and ranch with you, do you?"

He didn't like the questions she was asking. This was supposed to be time for her and him to get to know one another. Talk about the future sure, but their future. He didn't want to think about the boys getting older or the family breaking up as they take their own paths. He liked the way his life was right now. He had a wife and a chance for children. His brothers could find wives, too, and maybe build cabins on the property. The ranch was large enough to sustain several families.

But that was far off. After all, Bart and Andrew were only twenty, maybe twenty-one. He hadn't been looking toward getting a wife when he was that age. He was sure they weren't either. At that age, he had all his brothers to worry about. Perhaps if he hadn't, he would have been an old married man by now with his own children to worry over.

As soon as they walked into the parlor, it seemed each of his brothers had a question or request of his wife. The boys went up to bed at the same time and that was the end of his chance to speak with her privately. By the time they were all upstairs, she seemed exhausted. When he thought back on her day, he merely told her goodnight.

He probably should have taken this chance to kiss her. Nothing too grand. Merely a kiss on her forehead or peck on the cheek. Allow his arms to slide around her and they could have stood together for a couple of moments. Time for just the two of them.

He stared at the closed bedroom door. Too late now. She was probably already in bed. She had appeared tired by the time they finished the dishes. He enjoyed talking with her. Standing next to her in the kitchen—just the two of them as if they were an old married couple. He would need to find a way they could be together as a man and wife before they could become an old married anything. He knew what he should do, but he didn't want to rush her. Didn't want her to feel she needed to act like a wife so soon. They still hadn't spoken about themselves. Were they both going to get so involved in his brothers there wouldn't be time for them? No, he wouldn't let it get that bad. Lorelei belonged with him. He knew it deep down.

As he lay on his thrown-together sleeping area, his arms above his head, he thought he was lucky to have found her. And luckier that she fit in so well.

****

Lorelei sat in the parlor mending the pile of shirts and vests in front of her. Simon was lying on his stomach, his elbows out in front of him with an open book resting between his arms. "Sound out that last word. I think you can get it on your own."

"Why don't letters sound the same no matter where in the word they are?"

"Because America is made up of different people from all over the world and each one brought words with them that we use. Once you learn them, you'll not have problems sounding out various words. Now, let's try again." She pushed the wire-rimmed spectacles she wore for fine stitching back up her nose. They had been her fathers, so she was used to pushing them back on the bridge of her nose several times an hour.

"Do you think this was real? I mean this writer, this Jules Verne. Do you think he could have really done this?"

"The sign of a good writer is if they make the reader believe something is true or possible. Now read me more. I've only read this one once, and I find new things the more I hear a story."

"My friend Toby would like this book. He doesn't read as good as me…"

"As well as me…"

"What? Oh, he doesn't read as well as me, but he's fun to be around. We got things in common."

"In what ways?" She wanted to know more about this Toby if the boy had as much influence on Simon as she feared he did.

"He hasn't got a pa either. Died when he was little, same as me. He can fish, and he's the best frog catcher I ever been with. We caught a whole bunch, and then his ma fried the legs up for us. Best meal I ever ate." Then looking up guiltily changed his mind. "Until you got here, of course. Now you're the best cook."

"It isn't a contest, Simon. You can remember that as the best frog-leg meal you ever ate." She hid the smile that she felt play around her lips as he continued.

"I don't eat there often. I think they are kinda short on food 'cause Toby and me would snare rabbits, filch apples sometimes, and take them back to his house. His ma never asked where we got them. Just took them into the kitchen."

Lorelei was getting a sense of Toby's circumstances. "Are there other children?"

"He has a little brother and sister and an older sister, Hannah. She yells at us a lot and chases us out of the house most of the time. Says we're dirty and keep waking up the baby."

"Her baby?"

"Naw, her ma's, but she's always working in the fields and stuff."

"So they live out of town? On property like this one?"

"More of a farm. They only got one cow and some chickens."

"How about another chapter? There's time before supper." She listened with part of her attention, but much of it was thinking about Toby's family, especially the part about his father being dead for years while he had not one, but two younger siblings. And one only an infant.

Luke stood in the kitchen wearing damp socks

since there had been water spilled in front of the sink. He would have gone and changed out of them, but he treasured this time alone with his wife. He liked to draw it out, this easy camaraderie they had in the kitchen, but eventually, she always headed into the parlor with the others.

Once there, his brothers talked to her as if she was there for their amusement. He wanted her there for his amusement, wanted to get to know her and not through his brother's questions.

After she excused herself for the night, Luke was indecisive about following her right away or waiting as if his mind hadn't been on his wife all evening. Finally, he faked a yawn and told the others he was going up to bed.

No one lifted their eyes from their books or the chessboard as he moved on silent feet to his set of stairs. He would have to think of an excuse now to be bothering Lorelei after she had left them. Relieved to see the light shining under her door, he knocked lightly and waited anxiously for an answer.

The door opened a crack, and she stood there in a thin nightgown with the light from the candle outlining her body. He felt himself go rigid and his mouth felt dry.

"Ah, um-m-m, I thought we could take a minute and talk some."

She turned quickly letting the door swing open and giving him more of a view as she grabbed a knit shawl from the back of the chair to wrap around herself. He stepped in as she sunk to the edge of the bed appearing nervous. He hated that she was afraid of him or what he might do. He didn't mean to frighten her.

"I just came to socialize a little. We never get much time alone. Not even when we're doing dishes."

"The boys are becoming easier with me and feel they can ask me anything. I encourage them to do so, you know." She picked up her brush to finish what she evidently had been doing before he arrived.

"Let me help you." He took the brush from her unresisting hands and began to make long slow strokes, laying the hair smoothly along her back. He lifted the ends to make sure there weren't any snarls and continued at the roots again.

He saw her reflection in the mirror as she closed her eyes appearing to enjoy the pure indulgence of the brush against her scalp. He continued a few moments lost in her pleasure. Leaning down, he kissed her nape as he exposed it.

She tensed but didn't move or turn away. He took that as a good sign and sat next to her giving him more access to his wife. He was careful to move slowly, nipping and sucking along her neck tasting her skin gently. He wanted to do much more, be more aggressive with her, pleasure her, as he felt desire rise within him.

But he kept his hands on her arms, turning her enough so that he could reach her lips. Covering them with his own, the headiness of her response made his resolution not to do anything more tonight dissolve. He was becoming lost in the kisses, the pleasure of holding her, of having her lean toward him willingly.

He had made a decision, and he needed to keep to it. This was a time for them to get to know one another, but not in a physical sense. He feared if they did too much too fast, she would panic and flee. He tamped down his body's response and merely kissed her although he knew a moan escaped him at least once as he held his own passion in check.

"That's about all the socializing I can take, honey." He stood and tried to tug on his trouser front to give himself some relief in the confined space.

She gazed up at him, her eyes still dreamy and soft. "I liked what we were doing. Did I do something wrong? I don't understand."

"I'm not sure I do either about now, but I want to take things slow. We need to both be ready for the next step in our relationship. I need you to be sure before we commit to one another. There will be no goin' back after that." He moved toward the door. "Goodnight, Mrs. Foster."

She gave a shy smile. "Goodnight, Mr. Foster."

CHAPTER SIX

"Mayor Withers, how nice to see you. How is Mrs. Withers doing? That burn on her hand heal?" Lorelei walked to where the buggy carrying the mayor pulled up near her back stoop. When she heard the horse's hooves, she checked her appearance in the porch mirror as she came out to greet him.

"Yes, Miss Lorelei, she's doin' fine now. Hurt her some though for a day or two."

"You need me to ring the bell and see if Luke is close enough to come home?" She turned to reach for the leather strap on the bell used to call the boys in for supper or for any emergency when they are needed.

"No, I came to speak with you. It seems Hank's lawyers handling his affairs did a final tally and still had some money left over. The board decided since you came all this way, we should pay you a severance or something. It certainly wasn't your fault the fire happened and wiped out your livelihood." He was sweating in his three-piece suit, the tie wound around his neck pulled out as if he had tugged on it more than once. He looked around nervously as if he didn't want to be found there.

"It would have made a difference then, but I'm married and won't be going back to Cincinnati. Thank the board for me, and perhaps use it to start another library."

"Won't need to do that, neither. Those city lawyers bought an insurance policy for the library and books so everything we lost will be replaced 'cept maybe a few incidentals that were added as the building went up."

"Why, that's wonderful for the town. I can't believe it took them this long to notify you."

"Partly my fault since I didn't tell them about the fire right off. Then, by the time I did, we had all put the idea of ever having a library behind us. Now we can have one built within the year. You're still the best person who applied for the position. I thought the severance pay could keep you until the library opened again and then you'd have work. No one would think bad of you for wanting to live in town. I never thought you'd stay as long as you have once you saw the amount of work there was. Takin' care of a houseful of young men can't be too easy."

"No, not easy, but not as arduous as you might think. They are all good boys and try to lighten my load." She almost laughed aloud at his woebegone expression. He really thought she would leave her husband after almost a month just so the mayor wouldn't need to interview more potential librarians?

"Mayor, why don't you use that money to start a fund to buy newer firefighting equipment? That's something all the citizens should be able to get behind. Then if something like that happens again, the town will be more prepared. Safer."

"I'll make that suggestion to the board." He lifted the reins to get the team to move, but added, "I'm glad things worked out for you here. Luke's a fine man as I told you in town. I find I'm relieved I didn't mislead you."

"No, I feel beholden to you, Mayor. I might have missed finding this life if the library had managed not to burn."

He tipped his hat before setting the horses to turn and leave.

Luke kept watching her, his gaze following her around the room. It wasn't his usual hungry look, but there was something he was thinking about that made her uneasy. Was he sorry he married her? Sorry he was so precipitous in his offer now that he had time to think it over.

Trying to make herself useful, she kept out of the men's way so their life was more or less the same. Going to her room soon after dinner to give them time together as it had always been. What else could she do to be less intrusive?

She knew they all appreciated her cooking meals and packing lunches for them. She knew they liked having their clothes mended and clean ones available. They said they were pleased with how clean and neat things looked around the house. So why was Luke watching her like that? As if he were a bomb waiting to blow.

She excused herself to go to her room and read. There wasn't any more mending until someone damaged a garment, which left her with time for herself this evening. As she began to take the pins out of her hair, a knock sounded on the door. She called out for one of the boys to enter thinking someone needed help.

Surprisingly, Luke entered with his hands shoved into his front pockets and a mulish expression on his face. He began aggressively. "When were you gonna tell me?"

She tried to figure out what he was talking about. "I don't know…"

"Damn it, Lori, when were you going to tell me about the Mayor showing up here and offering you a job? In a note left on the table for all the boys to see?"

"Luke, I don't know what you're talking about. I just forgot, I guess. That was the day Paul came in with that big splinter and dinner almost burned while I worked on getting it out, and…I don't know. It wasn't important to me."

"Not important? We, I mean you and I, aren't important? I made a vow, and I expected you to treat it the same as I do."

"I did. I mean, I do." She was at a loss for words at his verbal attack. He had never been like this before, and he frightened her with the anger emanating from him. She felt defeated, crushed. "What do you want me to say?"

He slumped back against the closed door. "Just tell me when you're leaving. Maybe I can explain it to Simon and the twins. The others will understand."

She knew her brows drew down in worry, and she shook her head to emphasize her words. "Luke, I don't plan to leave. I made a vow, too, and I owe all of you loyalty for accepting me without knowing anything about me. You all have been so welcoming. I thought I was gaining a family."

His head snapped up and gazed into her eyes. "I did, too. Gaining a family, I mean. Having you here seems to fill a hole I didn't know we all felt since Ma passed on. I know the youngest are turning to you more and more for comfort. Something the rest of us have trouble dealing with."

"I take it someone said something to you in town this morning? And you've been fretting about it ever since?" She looked for any sign of emotion other than anger. She was disturbed that his good opinion of her mattered so much. This need could cause her more pain than comfort later in her life.

The mulish expression returned. "Not fretting exactly. Worried about the young 'uns and wondering how we'll all get on after having you around. Weren't you tempted to take the mayor up on his offer? I mean, it comes with a room and everything."

She chuckled, lightening the mood as she started counting off on each finger. "So does this one, but there is the added benefit of getting to do laundry and mending and ironing and cooking and cleaning and…"

His grin appeared along with the dimples. "All right—enough. You've proven you're irreplaceable in my home, in this family. You sure you don't want to leave and do the work I know you'd love to be doing?"

She was pleased he seemed interested. "I love books and reading which makes me a perfect librarian, but I can still read, get my hands on books, and help keep this family comfortable. I explained this to the mayor, and he understood. He said he felt he needed to offer the job to me first before putting the advertisement in the newspapers."

Luke watched her with a hard stare, his mouth mutinous and stubborn again. "You tell him that for real?"

She had to smile because he looked so much like Simon did when he wasn't winning an argument or getting his way. "Yes, for real. You are all stuck with me whether I burn dinner or scorch your shirts."

Taking a few steps to stand in front of her, he pulled her from the bed where she sat. "Then I want you to know today was the longest day of my life waiting for you to tell me you were leaving me. I guess I've gotten used to having you here when I get home each night, and I couldn't face a future where maybe you weren't here anymore."

"You should have asked immediately instead of having it fester. You probably gave yourself indigestion."

He nuzzled her neck, and she thought she felt the brush of his lips against her skin just under her right ear. "I'm feeling better now," he whispered. Then she did feel his lips as he nipped at her before sucking gently to end by licking it soothingly.

She tried not to shrug her shoulders and drive him away, but it tickled. He pulled away placing a quick kiss on her mouth as he stepped back. Her hand went to her lips, and he gave her a quick dimpled grin.

"See ya' in the mornin'."

She went to sleep wondering if he would ever take the next steps to make them man and wife. Was he waiting for her to say something? Ask? She felt she was nearing that moment if she could be sure he wouldn't turn her down.

Andrew sat at the kitchen table. His face screwed into a contorted grimace as Lorelei peeled potatoes. "They all look like wiggly marks. They make no sense to me. I'm just too stupid to read."

She took the chalkboard and wrote a few things then turned it back towards him. "Can you tell me what those mean?"

He squinted and said, "Oh, sure. That's the Circle K."

"And this." Her finger tapped the other symbol.

"That's the Rocking R. Why show me things I already know? I need to learn to read, so I can approach Sarah Ann's father and ask to court her. He's the minister, and I know he'll refuse if he finds out I can't read. He knows I left school at sixteen, so he may be lookin' for reasons to deny my request. I know she favors me, and I know I, ah, favor her."

"I know this is important to you, and that is why you are in here this afternoon instead of with the cattle. I don't think Sarah Ann would care about your ability to read or write, but I know you are missing out on a whole world of adventure and knowledge by not reading."

She tapped the board again. "I put these brands down because they are just like letters. Each letter makes a sound or along with another letter have a different sound. You already know that at times a C sounds like an S. Now, when it is in front of an H, the sound is different again."

"I'm never ever going to remember all of this. I can't do it, Lorelei, I just can't do it."

"Let's try the book again. No one is coming home for a while yet, so we have plenty of time."

Andrew picked up the book with a determined expression on his face, his lips firmed. He pushed his arms straight and then brought the book closer, getting himself ready to read aloud which was extremely difficult for him, she knew. He stared at the page, moving the book a couple of times before tentatively beginning. "Call me Ish-ish-mek? I don't know the next word."

"Call me Ishmael. It's been a while since I read *The Whale*. Spell it out for me."

"S—no, B, and maybe another A or C…"

She glanced up in time to catch him moving the book away from him again. "Just a minute, Andrew." She rose and went to her sewing basket which she had used earlier. Taking her father's magnifying spectacles, she slipped the thin, wire arms over each of her brother-in-law's ears. "Try these."

His eyes opened wider, and he set the book at an angle on the table. "I can see the difference between an A and an E. I didn't realize it was so easy to tell the difference. All these letters, they show up now."

"You're farsighted like my father. Your reading difficulties are due to you not seeing the differences in the letters, not in not knowing how to read. That's why signs and things in big print you could read. Keep the spectacles and practice reading. I think you'll find you'll pass any test the minister can give you before allowing you to court Sarah Ann."

"I hope so. This has given me hope I might stand a chance with her."

That evening after supper, Lorelei waited for Luke's knock on her bedroom door. She had been looking forward to this time between them each night. After she tucked Simon into bed, left the older boys playing chess or reading in their room, and Matt in the workshop next to the barn, no one would need to speak with Luke.

The knock and the door opening came simultaneously. She glanced up expectantly and was rewarded by her husband's hot gaze. She had thought of offering him the opportunity to sleep next to her in bed, but then always felt it wasn't the right time. After all, they had been married over a month and knew she should be ready. She only wished she knew what held her back.

He stood in front of her, and she knew she wanted to feel his arms around her, if nothing more. She always felt safe and secure in his arms, listening to his heartbeats as they leaned against one another. He had begun to kiss her goodnight each evening which she took comfort in as well.

Lifting her face up for her kiss, his mouth came down over hers. Something happened between them. Something kept his mouth covering hers as he pulled her tighter to him. Both of them taking and receiving. She felt the brush of his tongue across her lips and sighed, opening like a flower blossoming.

Their bodies aligned with one another's, and their mouths fused. She tried pulling him closer and resented she hadn't been in her nightgown already. That she wasn't closer to his body that she knew was hard for her. She wanted to be taken down onto that coverlet and have him make her his wife completely. This was the closest they had come, and she knew there wasn't any reason not to be as husband and wife. Not to put off the inevitable any longer.

She felt him lower her to the mattress, felt his buttons beneath her fingers as she began helping him undress. As she felt his desire for her through her skirts, she was frantic to feel his bare skin against hers. With his body over hers and his hand on a breast, she was impatient for him to get on with it. She wanted to feel all of him become part of her.

From somewhere in the desire-induced fog, a small voice called out. "Lorelei?" Then again. "Lorelei? My belly hurts. I don't feel good."

Luke's head dropped to her shoulder as he tried reining in his harsh breaths. The sound rushed in her ear, but through it all, she knew what she had heard first.

Simon was at the base of the stairs calling up to her. He needed her, and Luke knew what her answer would be to the young boy. "I'm coming, Simon. How many of those plums did you eat this afternoon?"

She wiggled out from under Luke as he rolled onto his back with a moan. She saw the slight smile on his lips and knew he was accepting this interruption as he did all his brothers' disruptions.

He said, shaking his head and chuckling, "I'll take care of him. Give me a minute."

She began to see the humor as well. "No, you need to work in the morning. I'll help him. This may take a little while to pass." Rising from the mattress, she liked what she saw. Her husband on her bed where she was so sure he should be. Maybe not tonight or even tomorrow night—but one night, soon. They will become husband and wife, and it would be worth the wait.

Lorelei waved to Dorothy as soon as she entered the store, but her friend was helping a large man at the counter. She continued to the rear of the store area hoping it would provide what she was looking for.

Picking up a pair of brown trousers, she held them up to her own body, sticking her leg out to judge the length. She wasn't sure so turned to a lone woman shopping in the next aisle. "Excuse me. Do these look like they would fit a fifteen-year-old boy? Almost sixteen?"

The woman looked up startled and glanced around in all directions to see if there was someone else Lorelei was speaking to. Finding only the two of them, the woman answered. "The Foster twins? I'd get the next size up. At that age, they'll be shooting up inches in a year. They can roll them up for now. My Toby's growing so fast..."

Lorelei had become used to the small-town way of people knowing who she was while she had no idea who they were. They all seemed friendly except that Madeline who she hadn't seen again since her trip in with Matthew. And this woman hardly seemed the same sort. Shy but pleasant looking, she seemed to try to melt into the background. Her brown dress was plain without buttons and her woven straw hat's silk flowers were faded from years in the sun. Just as she was about to make the woman's acquaintance, the other woman scurried away and out the door leaving only the sound of the chime in her wake.

Dorothy approached and whispered, "Don't let Helen's actions hurt your feelings or anything. She's skittish around most of us."

"Most of us?"

"Yes, the women in town. Some haven't been very nice to her since they're afraid their husbands might wander down to her farm, I guess. We talk a little when she comes in, but she sticks to herself for the most part. Did you find what you needed?"

"Yes, I want to get the twins into more presentable

clothes so they will attend church with Andrew, Simon, and me. It's fine for Simon to be in bib overalls at his age, but the others are old enough for trousers. And add a couple of shirts for Luke so he can pass his down to the twins."

"I don't envy you keeping those boys dressed and fed. Must seem like the same day over and over again."

"It changes a little bit." Lorelei found herself thinking about Toby's mother. "Dorothy, I'm not asking to gossip, but what can you tell me about Helen. She seemed sad and alone."

"She and her husband, Bill, bought a farm closest to town to the east. It's furthest from the river so never grew good crops if we had a dry year. They worked it for two or three years. They had a couple of children, and then her husband gets sick. It was a long, drawn-out time of it before he died. That probably did the most damage to the fields. You know, leaving them like that and letting the wild take over again."

"She had no family? No one could help?"

Dorothy shook her head sadly. "No one had time to take on another's fields and such. Everyone was getting established. Remember this was eight or so years ago. She's been raising those kids on her own, and if that meant welcoming a few lonely men to her bed, then she did what she had to do to keep food on the table. I don't hold no blame. She does the best she can for all of them, even the youngest."

"That story breaks my heart. I want to help…"

"She has her pride, mind you. I sometimes discount some of the food she buys." Dorothy put the items in a crate. "Tell her it's on sale or a special order that got left. She may know, but never says so. I understand.

She's already lost her good name, so what else is there left if not her pride?"

"You're a good woman, Dorothy, and I'll be right back for these." Lorelei wasn't sure if it was because she had come so close to being in this woman's shoes or if she was naturally unable to accept children being in need. Either way, she left the store in search of the other woman. She wasn't sure what she would say to her, but she knew she couldn't let Helen go without some offering of friendship.

Seeing the faded, brown skirt disappear around a corner, Lorelei hurried to catch up with it. She needn't have rushed. Helen stood flat against the white clapboard wall of the butcher shop. Her eyes clenched closed as if not seeing anyone would keep them from seeing her as well.

Lorelei began, "Helen, I'm afraid I don't know your family name. I wanted to ask a favor."

The woman's eyes snapped open meeting Lorelei's. "I don't think you understand the circumstances…"

"I know my brother, Simon, misses seeing your son. I understand Toby is quite a fisherman and the best frog catcher in the county. I would love to have him come out to the ranch and spend the day or two. Simon is regretting his long absence from school."

"Mrs. Foster, do you think he can convince Toby to go back to school? I mean, I need him around the farm, but he needs the education, too. The farm work can wait till I get to it myself."

"I am having Simon return to school. He won't have a voice in the matter. If the schoolmaster is the reason these students are quitting, then I will go before the school board and fight tooth and nail for better treatment. For all the students."

"I'm glad Simon has you on his side. He always seemed so lost, like he was forgotten by the others."

"I think with him so much younger and the ranch so demanding, Simon was left to raise himself. But I'm here now, and he will have to find out what having a mother is like. He may rue the day I showed up."

The other woman smiled. "I don't think he will. He always impressed me as being a smart little boy."

"Then it's settled? Toby can come to us one day and you'll have Simon one day? Don't be afraid to give him work to do. He has chores he does at home, and he can do them just as well at your place."

"I can't thank you en—"

"That's right, Helen. You can't thank me. Just stand strong when those boys try to talk their way out of going to school."

Helen nodded and put out her hand for Lorelei to shake. They said their goodbyes as they made final arrangements for the boys to meet.

Simon watched Lorelei closely as she shucked peas, while he should have been doing the homework she gave him right after breakfast. Then he looked enviously outside to the morning sunshine. She tapped the chalkboard to bring his attention back to the multiplication problems written on it.

Raising her eyebrows, she asked, "Do you need help?"

"No, just wondering how often you have to shave to stay so soft."

"I, I, uh, women don't need to shave. We don't

have beards as men do."

"Except Miss Jenkins. She was our old teacher, and she had a mustache kinda like an otter I saw once."

"Well, even if a woman does have facial hair, one does not mention the fact—to anyone."

He continued to stare, so she stopped and turned to him. "What is it that has your curiosity, Simon?"

"I know you're soft. So, you just wake up every morning that way? I mean, I know Luke and Mark shave, and they still get prickly by the end of the day. When they tucked me into bed, it would scratch."

The last remark caught her attention, her curiosity. "When did they stop tucking you into bed?"

"I don't know. When I got too old, I guess."

"But you're not too old for me to tuck you in?"

"No, you're like a ma, and mas tuck their kids in bed till they're grown and gone."

"Then I will continue to tuck you in until you tell me you are too old, but I hope that won't be too soon since I like the quiet time together."

"Like this." He nodded and shyly went back to his chalkboard.

"Yes, just like this. I'm here, and you can always ask me anything, and I will try to answer you honestly."

He turned his head and gazed up through his lashes. "That's what a ma does, too. Toby's ma always answers honestly even if he doesn't want to hear it."

Simon returned to printing numbers on the chalkboard. Lorelei thought about their conversation. The boy knew what a mother should do, should be, and he knew he had missed it. His thinking of her as a mother swelled her heart with pride and love. She may not have been part of this family for long, but she loved each and every one in it. She surprised herself because she thought of herself as self-reliant, contained, and in control. Now she was dependent on these boys, all of them, for her comfort, her feeling of home.

She glanced up just as Simon saw who was at the back door. He jumped up, the chalkboard clattering to the table noisily. "Toby! How did you get here?"

"I walked. That's why I'm kinda late."

"Come in, and get a drink, Toby. I'm Mrs. Foster, but you can call me Lorelei as Simon does."

"Ma said I was to call you Mrs. Foster, so if it's just the same to you, I'll do as my ma says."

"I understand, Toby. Simon, you're free to go and play."

"C'mon, Toby. We can find the kittens in the barn. The mother keeps moving them every time I find her nest."

Lorelei watched as the two ran towards the barn. She smiled at their happiness in one another's presence. It hadn't taken her long to decide Toby was a good boy. He wouldn't be a bad influence on Simon and could already see why the two were drawn to one another. In fact, she could see where they would be good for one another.

Both were about the same age and size, so they met on equal footing. They both had admirable traits the other found worthy of envy. She thought they had about the same level of education, so she was willing to tutor Toby if he needed it to catch up with his classmates at school. Both had had to grow up with less than both parents and had done a good job of it so far.

Lorelei felt she could help them both back onto the right path that would ensure their future as educated, well-adjusted adults. All she had to do was figure out how to go about doing that without her husband knowing. She wasn't sure how he would take her using the family's resources toward helping others. She had been trying not to be alone with Luke in case she lost nerve and told him everything. No husband she knew would let her do what she planned on doing.

CHAPTER SEVEN

"Lorelei, pack a change of clothes. I've told Matt he's in charge until I get back." She watched as Luke began opening cupboard doors and putting food items into a cloth sack marked cornmeal.

"Where are we going, Luke? What food do you want? Are we going camping?" She tried to think of everything she would need, but he seemed to have ideas of his own.

"Not really, but it's one of my favorite places ever since I was small. Come on, we should get going so we can enjoy the afternoon sunshine."

"Who is going to cook for the rest of the boys?"

"The pantry is chuck-full. Matt or Bart can both make something decent out of what you've got in there. And the icehouse has a full side of beef in it."

Rushing upstairs, she left her husband to pack ground coffee and a crock of butter. If he had given her a warning, she could have made up meals and left them along with the fresh bread. She just baked several loaves but could have left more if she had known.

Luke's voice called up, "Get a move on it, Lorelei. I'm anxious now, and I don't want any cow stuck in the mud or bull with a boil to stop us. Do you need me to carry anything down?"

She appeared at the top of the steps with a full pillowcase. "You did say just one change of clothing, didn't you? And personal items like brush and tooth powder?"

"Yep, that should be all we'll need. Bring a cape or coat since it gets cool in the evenings where we're going. I got the food."

"Are you sure? Do you want me to go over what you have?"

"No, the horses are ready out back."

"Horses? We're to go by horse? Luke, I don't know how to ride a horse."

His face was comical, the disbelief plain. "I, ah, I'll help you. It isn't a difficult ride, and I chose a quiet horse for you."

Matt tried to hide his grin as he overheard them from the back porch. "Leave it to my brother to not know his wife didn't ride. This should be an interesting trip." He helped her up and fit the stirrups to her leg showing her how to hook her heels against the wooden bottom. Then he explained how to hold the reins and gave one to Luke who had tied the sacks to his saddle.

"Luke will take your horse's leads, so you won't have to worry about it taking you back to the barn."

She looked aghast at the animal with its eyelids half-closed. "She'd do that? On purpose?"

"She would only go back to the barn to get to her oats." Luke yelled at his brother, "Matt, quit teasing her or so help it I'll…"

By now Matt was laughing. "I'm sorry, Lorelei. Buttercup here wouldn't hurt a fly. Too lazy to swing her tail. She'll get you there, but it would be best if Luke pulled her, otherwise she'll stay in one place munching grass and hoping for a treat."

Blowing air out through his lips making a sound

much like a horse, Luke kicked his mount into motion. Buttercup hesitated with her neck stretched out until her feet followed. She was easy to stay on, so Lorelei held on tightly to the saddle horn and tried to move with the horse as Matt had suggested.

Luke looked back often, and every once in a while, called to ask if she was still all right. She answered she was and didn't expand on the fact the excitement of riding had left her long ago.

The air was cooler as they climbed in elevation. In fact, it got so cold she thought she saw snowflakes, but that couldn't be possible since it was July, and it couldn't snow in July.

Luke stopped and walked back to her, tugging the cape out of her pack. "You need to put this on. Don't remove your gloves, and if we get into an area where visibility is zero, stay with the horse. She's warm and will help keep you alive."

She smiled but thought it was an odd thing to joke about. "Luke, why are you saying this?"

"Those clouds are snow clouds, or rain if we luck out and the temperature warms. But I don't think we'll be that fortunate. We're closer to the summer cabin than the ranch. We need to keep going and hope the snow holds off until we get there."

He wrapped a blanket around her after, asking if she brought a shawl or any other clothing before topping it with her cape. At least it had a hood and she snuggled down into it, but she remembered what Luke said, how he looked when she last saw his face.

It hit them quickly, so quickly she couldn't believe how warm it had been when they left the ranch and now how deep the snow was piling up as the horses trudged through it. The sleet hit her face like stinging thistles. The horses' heads dropping as their ears lay back.

She closed her lids to the freezing air burning her eyes. Breathing from beneath her cloak, she didn't want the cold air to cool her body. She looked ahead and saw only a sheet of white, no cabin or any sign of a trail.

She prayed Luke knew the area well enough to find the cabin he spoke of in this storm. She couldn't have kept going if not for his strength and stamina that had both horses continuing to move. Lorelei hoped Luke had a warm coat and gloves. He didn't have when he was bundling her up, but his safety was essential to both their lives. He wouldn't be so foolish as to not take care of himself, would he?

She couldn't even see the rear end of his horse. Only the fact Buttercup's reins were taut gave her confidence Luke was still in his saddle, still heading to the cabin he indicated would be their safe destination.

Then she began feeling sleepy even though she tried to lift her head twice to peek through the small opening she allowed herself in her hood. She felt herself slump forward remembering Matt's admonishment to hold on to the horn. Her hand felt numb, and she wasn't sure if it was due to having held the horn for so long or if it was frozen in place.

The horse stopped, and her first fear was that Luke had fallen and was laying hurt on the frozen ground, being covered by the snowflakes still falling so densely. Suddenly, a dark blur emerged from the white, and she stopped a scream knowing it wouldn't help anything.

Someone grabbed and hauled her off the saddle, Luke's voice close to her ear as he carried her. "Lori? Lori, honey, talk to me. Don't go to sleep, sweetheart."

She felt a difference in the wind, and then the sound quieted. Feeling her feet touch a hard surface, she finally opened her eyes. The snow was frozen to his whiskers and his hat and hair. He looked like a snowman come to life.

"Luke? Are we home?" She was aware of being inside a building, and as she gazed around, he bent down to light the fire already made up in the stove. The flames crackled to life, and he stood again.

"Take off this cape. Everything you're wearing is frozen right now but will thaw and be soaking wet in a couple of minutes. Let me help you."

He started on the ties beneath her arm, and she pushed his hands away. "I can do it."

He looked down at her worriedly. "All right."

Then he grabbed a broom and went out the rear door, the howl of the wind and snow took the opportunity to enter the cabin landing on the floor and remaining there. Melting in the still cold room.

She knew he was right about taking off her clothes. She knew they were wet through but hesitated. Her mind wasn't as frozen as the rest of her. Being without clothing didn't seem like the right choice.

"I swept a path to the privy and knocked down all the webs. It's so cold, though, I would think any spider was holed up somewhere warmer." Then she watched as he went to a large trunk against one wall and pulled out furs. She recognized a buffalo hide, and she thought the others were bearskins. Luke threw them onto the mattress of the only bed before saying, "Now get naked. I mean it, Lori, or we might not make it. Skin to skin contact is the only thing that will keep us from freezing right now."

She thought she nodded but wasn't sure. Her fingers were so cold she couldn't maneuver the buttons through the holes. Her feet were numb, and she feared he was right. She began shivering so hard she couldn't speak.

"I have to care for the horses." He grabbed his still-frozen gloves, pushing his hands into them before going through the side door. She heard the horses out there, probably colder and more miserable than she was.

The fire gave off little heat, although any was like manna. Pulling her damp dress over her head, she sat on the edge of the bed, bending to untie her boots with difficulty. Her hands still didn't want to obey her mental orders to do more. Wet stockings and camisole were finally pulled off. She tried to lay them out on the chairs to dry but found it too much of a trial.

With the removal of the last of the items, she lifted the top pile of fur and crawled in. That's when the real shaking and shivering began and when her fingers and feet began tingling and prickles covered her skin.

She tried to ignore her discomfort. Tried to concentrate on the feel of the fur and how its softness encompassed her limbs. The shivering lessened, and slowly her body eased, but the sharp skin pricks continued as shudders racked her body.

Feeling the bear rug move, Luke entered her bed. She felt his body shuddering with the cold, with reaction to what little warmth she had put off in the time she was wrapped in the furs. She reached over to him knowing his fingers and feet would be colder than even hers were.

Unknowing how much longer he stayed outside to care for the horses, however long it was, she had been inside and enjoying the heat from the fire and the warmth building up under these covers.

"Come here, share my warmth, Luke."

He hesitated, but then allowed her to pull close to him. Shakes shuddered through him in spasms. Just as she thought he was warm, his body shuddered, and he let out a deeply-held breath. She stroked his body, held his cold hands, which she tried to warm against her, and kept her feet against his as if she were hot bricks to his cold ones.

"D-don't, Lori, I'll make you cold, again."

"No, I'm warmer, and I can share. Please, don't try to pull away. You need to get warm for both our sakes. I won't make it without you."

"Th-the s-snow's stopped. You'll be f-fine now once the s-sun melts it. Th-the horses will take you d-down the mountain t-to the ranch if you give th-them their head."

"I'm not going anywhere without you. We'll both get home. Now lie here, and get warm. I'm so tired, let's just rest for a while before deciding what to do."

Snuggling tightly against his body, her hand lay on his hair-covered chest, the fine hairs feeling comforting in the darkness of the cabin. The glow through the stove's vents the only source of light. She heard his soft even breathing just before she fell asleep.

Lori woke to his hand stroking the length of her body repeatedly. The rough pads of his fingers coarse against her skin. Pressing into him as she stretched, she allowed her body to uncoil from the curved position she had maintained for too long.

His mouth touched the side of her face and then

traveled to her lips. He nipped and sucked before covering her mouth completely pushing his tongue inside and touching hers tentatively. She enjoyed his attentions and responded by seeking his mouth in the same manner, a moan coming from deep in his throat.

His voice rumbled through her body. "Are you feeling all right? Anything hurt or burn?"

"I, ah, I think my muscles are sore from riding. I mean, I only feel it when I move certain ways."

"H-m-m-m-m, let me see if this helps."

Both his hands found one thigh as he kneaded her muscles much like she would do with bread dough. Wanting to moan and groan it felt so good, but instead, she lay quiet beneath his ministrations. When she was about to cry out with the pleasure of it, he moved to the other thigh and gave the same treatment.

"Is that better?" he purred. Something soft and warm about his voice making her want to lay flat and allow him full access to her body.

"Much. Is there something I can do for you?"

"You're already doing it. I can hardly keep my hands off the rest of you."

Feeling he could do no wrong and feeling generous towards him, she urged him to do more. Let her feel more. "Then don't try. This is what we came up here for, isn't it? What we nearly died trying to accomplish?"

He stopped moving, stopped breathing. "Is it what you want, though? I wanted us to get to know one another, possibly more, without the interruptions we run into at home."

"I knew what you had in mind. I think it's time we move to the next step, if you do."

"I think about nothing else. It's just that I thought we would know one another better first. Not that I'm not ready to be your husband, but I told you I would wait till we knew one another better."

"I think I know enough about you right now. You're my husband, you care about me, and you protected me. It's enough for now."

"So, I should stop. We know enough about each other already?" She heard the strain and uncertainty in his voice.

"I think we know enough about each other to become husband and wife in the carnal way."

"Oh-h-h, you don't know how relieved I am to hear that."

"I can imagine…"

His hand began moving across her abdomen in little circles spirally outward until it brushed over the thatch of hair on her mound. Returning to the spot, she tensed, but didn't forbid the touch. His lips opened over hers again. Entering her mouth, his tongue dueled with hers. Cupping her mound, he slid a finger into her most private of places. She knew enough about sex to know this was all part of the final activity.

He moaned as his finger slid into her deeper. "You're so silky, so smooth I can hardly keep from being overeager. I don't want to hurt you, but my body wants to be joined with yours, inside yours. I don't know how to be gentle, and I don't want to be rough."

She didn't know how to answer him. She felt her hips rise to him, urging him to do something more. "I'm not afraid. I know you won't intentionally hurt me. You'd never hurt me. It's not in you to hurt anyone."

"This is different, animal-like. I want to claim you

now that we're here, but you've never done this have you?"

"No, but it's a natural urge. The one to mate. So I'm prepared for anything."

He kissed her again, taking her lips, sucking and pushing his tongue to hers. His hand began a rhythmic motion until it was Lorelei who couldn't get enough, feel enough. She began to kiss him aggressively, urging him to faster and stronger strokes.

Pulling her under him, he rested between her legs. Soothing her with his hands, he let her feel him between her thighs at the opening that was as hungry for him as he seemed for her. He thrust and stopped, waiting for something, but she thrust upwards with her hips and instigated a fury of pumping from him.

She felt his weight, the roughness of his hair-covered legs against her softer ones, the pressure as he pushed into her, and the release as they pulled apart. Then the frenzied activity as she tried to remain close to him while he retracted and surged into her repeatedly.

All she saw were sparks and lightning bolts behind closed eyelids. A tremor raced through her body, exited through her fingertips, and made her toes curl. How could she feel all these things and live through them? Perhaps that was it. This was her death, and she was feeling all the pleasure and good that would have been hers if she had lived to be ninety.

Luke collapsed on top of her. Quiet and deathly calm. Was it the same with him? Had he felt that cataclysmic ecstasy, also? Was that what women never discussed? What men teased one another about? If it was, they were in trouble because she liked it. She liked it a whole lot. No wonder his folks had seven children.

This could be very addictive.

Kissing her, he took the weight off her with his forearms. "Did I hurt you? I tried not to lose control, but somewhere along the way, I think I did. I'm sorry if I hurt you, honey."

"You didn't hurt me. I was right there with you the whole time. It was more than I ever understood happened. I didn't know any of this, not really, only the general biological functions."

He chuckled. "I never thought about the 'general biological functions.' I just know it felt great, and once we were joined, nothing was going to stop me from making love to you." He saw her duck her head and avert her eyes from him. "I'm sorry. I never felt this way before, Lori. Believe me when I tell you this was different for me—more intense, more passionate."

He stroked his rough palm up and down her arm.

"Perhaps it's due to opportunity, Luke. I mean, I was here, and we had just gone through a frightening experience. Perhaps if you had been to town more recently, this wouldn't have happened at all."

He narrowed his eyes at the term he and his older brothers used to mean a certain event. "I had the opportunity every time I went to town but passed it by once we were married. That isn't what this is. It's not the same with you. It's been different right from the start. It wasn't like me to go up to a pretty woman on the street even if she was crying. I didn't think twice about approaching you and trying to make things right for you."

"You think I'm pretty? Really, Luke?" There were tears glistening in her eyes.

"You're beautiful. Why do you doubt it? You have

the loveliest hazel eyes, both the color and shape. They kind of tip up like on the outside. I love to watch you laugh with the boys because they just sparkle. And when you're up to something, they give you away." She hid her face with her hand, but he continued. "I probably shouldn't have told you that because now you'll be able to hide things from me."

"I'll never hide things from you, Luke. Nothing that really matters. Why would I ever want to?" She watched him, her honesty plain on her face.

"And I'll never 'go to town.' I'll never be untrue to you." He kissed her and then pulled away from her, although his hand remained on one part or another of her body as they talked.

Lorelei asked what seemed to matter most. "Matt told me about your parents, what he remembered. What was it like for you? You accepted the brunt of the work and worry for the entire family."

He rolled a length of her hair around one finger acting as if they were discussing nothing more important than what to have for supper. "I was sixteen when Pa fell off the barn roof. I told him I could do it, but he always wanted to do things himself to make sure that it got done to his satisfaction. I was on the ground sending him shingles up with a pulley system."

"He fell, and you were the first one there."

He nodded thinking of the long-ago day. The regret of allowing his pa up on the roof alone without tying him to a safety rope. His inability to hold the rope when his pa made a wild grab for the pulley. The crumpled body of his father lying in the dust at the foundation to the barn.

All of it, he could have prevented all of it if he had

been stronger with his father. Refused to help without the safety rope. Done the job himself. So many ways to change that day if he had only known the outcome of allowing his pa to do something his own way.

"You two were too much alike. Tell me he didn't always want to do the difficult things, the dangerous work. Keep the others safely at a distance."

He furrowed his brow. "What are you talking about? I let the boys help, make sure work gets divided. They all have to know how to do everything around a ranch."

"Like pulling a heifer out of the mud without breaking its leg or endangering the rescuer. Birthing a breech calf or lancing a boil on a bull's nether regions."

He felt a blush suffuse his face, embarrassed she knew how he had taken on tasks to prevent his brothers from possible injury. "They'll learn soon enough. No reason to get them hurt when I can do it myself safely. Then they'll know how to do it themselves someday."

"Just as your father taught you?"

He nodded thinking of how he and his pa taught the same way. How Pa took Matt and him out to the range, from branding to everything else as soon as they could manage to stay on a horse. He was too much like his pa, but he found he wanted it that way.

"And your mother? Did she really give up on you with Simon so young?"

"She got a cough one winter and just couldn't kick it. I'm not sure she had the fight in her to do so. It's not that she didn't love us, but she loved Pa more and wanted to be with him.

"She knew she left the boys in good hands. That I would care for them." He felt her pick up his hand and kiss the palm then hold it against her cheek.

"Don't feel sorry for me, Lori. I had great parents and have great brothers. I didn't miss out on my childhood or anything that romantic. I had the childhood I wanted, and I have the life I want now. I worry at times having the responsibilities of the boys, sure, but it doesn't keep me awake at night. Doesn't make me think I could have had more if things had been different." He lay to her side and placed one arm under his head. "I would have been in the same place if Pa had lived."

"I think you're right, Luke. You were made to be a rancher, but maybe some of your brothers want other things. More education, wives of their own."

"Of course, they will. I was just contemplating the best places to build them homes of their own when the time comes. The ranch can support more families and as the boys marry, we'll expand the number of cattle and the acreage under till."

"What if they want more than what you can give them? Some may want to leave, but that doesn't mean they want to leave the family. That they don't support you and agree with what you did and when you did it. They understand you only wanted the best thing for the family at the time."

He sat up, letting the fur slip off his shoulders and the cool air enter their comfy nest. He was concerned with her questions. "Did one of them say something? Someone unhappy with how I'm running things?"

"No, not at all. I've always been pleased at how well you all live together without rancor or blame. I would never have believed that seven men could live together without more arguments or fights. You are inspirational."

She kissed him—a long, slow kiss using her tongue as he had on her. He was more than willing to allow her license to experiment on his body. It didn't take long before his body took lead, showing her ways to enjoy one another while giving pleasure.

He slipped back under the furs and made sure she knew where he wanted to be and what he wanted to be doing.

CHAPTER EIGHT

The stomping in the stable attached to the cabin wasn't made by hungry horses. His brother's voice called through the open back door. "Luke, sorry for interrupting your, um, trip. I'm frozen to the bone, so I gotta come in."

Luke's eyes popped open to see Lori's eyes filled with surprise and fear. He kicked out of the furs leaving them covering his still-naked wife as he pulled on his trousers. "Matt, what the hell you doin' here? Something happen at the ranch?"

His brother entered, pulling off his gloves and going straight to the fire burning in the stove near the center of the room. Squatting down, he put his hands near the heat. "I could handle anything that happened down there. I rode all the way up here because I was afraid you two got caught in the blizzard. We could see it come across the ridge from the ranch house. Wasn't sure you made it all the way here since you were pullin' Buttercup. Didn't think you could outrun the storm."

"We didn't. It came upon us pretty fast, and neither of us had the clothing to be in weather like that. I was planning a picnic on the way up, maybe a trip to the river to see the salmon and trout."

Matt glanced to the pile of furs on the bed, then looked up grinning. "Quite the dashing courtship you were planning. Snowstorm didn't seem to prevent the rest of your plans from seeing satisfaction."

A squeak of maidenly modesty rose from the hump in the bedding.

Matt threw the comment over his shoulder. "Come on out, Lorelei. You've got nothing I haven't seen before, after all. I know what love bites look like."

A groan of humiliation sounded from the bearskin.

Matt's eyes twinkled with humor, and Luke felt wary of letting him closer to the bed. Matt sat down on the side of it and continued to talk as if he'd heard nothing. "So how's the honeymoon coming?" Then, turning to Luke asked, "I mean the poor thing can still walk, can't she? Remember she has to straddle Buttercup all the way home after this."

A low moan of what sounded like complete mortification escaped the furs.

"Enough, Matt, she's not used to having brothers teasing her like this. You've seen us, and you can go back and tell the others we're both fine."

"I haven't actually seen you both." At this, Luke stepped forward, but Matt raised his hands' palms outward and, still laughing, said, "I'm content to know you both made it safely, but I can't leave yet. My horse needs to rest, and I need to warm up. Do you have any food, or were you planning on living on love?"

Another low moan.

"You can have some of the corn bread I brought up here, and then you are heading home. Take my horse, he's well rested, and you won't need to waste so much time here." Luke spoke firmly, and his eyes warned of dire consequences if his brother continued to tease Lori.

Matt gave a pat to the top of the furs. "Sounds good to me. Like I said, I was hoping you made the cabin, but I came in case you got stuck on the trail. I brought food just in case, too." He went back to the stove, pulling some ham and cheese wrapped in butcher paper out of his coat pocket. "Lorelei, you're gonna get hot hiding under there, and you're gonna have to face me some time. You may as well be comfortable while I'm here."

Luke made a fist, and Matt's eyes widened in mock surprise before pouring himself a cup of coffee. He stayed about half an hour before saying he was ready to leave.

"I'll let the rest know how I found you. Well, not how I found you. I'll let them know you're both safe." Glancing at Luke, he softened his voice. "I'm glad you're getting along with Lorelei, really I am. Don't hurry home. We can do for ourselves for a while longer."

Over his shoulder, Luke called out as he was ushering his younger brother out the door, "Lori, feel free to come out and get some air. Matt won't be back in here before he leaves." Then to his brother he added, "I'll help you saddle up."

Matt called back from the horse stalls, "You mean you want to see the last of me as quickly as you can."

Hearing the door open, then close, Lorelei let out another huff of warm breath. She was suffocating under all these furs but couldn't face Matthew and his ill-timed sense of humor. She trusted Luke, though, so pushed the heavy covers off her head inhaling the cooler cabin air.

She pulled her dress on over her head before stepping out and slipping on her boots. She needed to use the privy, the urgency growing more severe as

Matthew had sat and said things that still made her cringe when remembering them.

She reentered the cabin at the same time Luke came from the other door. She stared at the scuffed wood floorboards, not knowing how to look at the man who had given her such physical pleasure. Who she had allowed such liberties.

"Lori, Matt was only teasing. He won't say anything one way or the other to the boys."

"I know, but he's right. Everyone will know what we've been doing."

"Everyone thought we were doing this already. Most married people do."

She heard the humor in his voice, and she felt worse for the guilt. "How do women face anyone after this?"

"How do you think either of us came about? Our parents did the same sort of things."

"I know. Matthew and I spoke of the same thing one time."

His brows drew down as if contemplating that possible conversation. "How did this subject come up between the two of you?"

She could tell he was angry but wasn't sure she could explain. "Simply how one does not wish to think about one's parents, um, being intimate, although, of course, one is the proof of such intimacies." She tried not to look at him as she kicked off her boots. "It was actually less embarrassing talking to him about it than explaining it to you."

She saw his grin and dimples appear. "So what do you think of such intimacies now? More acceptable to you?"

She felt herself blush and nodded. "I understand the attraction." She pulled the dress off quickly and jumped under the covers again.

Luke added more logs to the fire and moved the pot closer before slipping his trousers off, lifting the edge of the bearskin and sliding in next to her. "Do you think we should stop? Will you be able to face the boys easier if we deny what we feel for one another?" His hand slowly stroked her body, caressing all her curves and planes.

Her eyes closed as she enjoyed his touch. "No, this has nothing to do with the boys. With anyone except the two of us. I admit I never understood what went on between a husband and wife. What I've discovered is something new and wonderful and more than I thought possible. I thought it would be more like a duty. A means to beget children. It is so much more, and I don't think it would be the same if there weren't true feelings between us. I think we were meant to be together."

"So, you think the fire was fate? That you arriving on that day in that manner was meant to be? So we would end up together?"

"I think fate had a part in it. I also think I felt safe with you. I don't know why. After all, we were strangers, and I'm usually much more wary. I didn't come from a small town where everyone is trustworthy. Even without the mayor's urging, I knew you would be right for me."

Chuckling, he asked, "Nothing to do with lusting after me?"

She buried her head. "I can't think of that now."

"Then don't think at all." He lifted her onto his stiff erection and began to move beneath her slowly. "Just feel. You make me very, very happy, and I make you very, very happy, and that's all that counts. Don't let what others think of you or about you rule your life. We do this for one another, and that's all that matters."

She threw her head back and relaxed. Rocking as he set the rhythm for them. Finally, they both met a climactic end, their orgasms draining them into a deep sleep once again.

Lorelei felt him move, leave the bed as the warmth dissipated with his body heat. She opened her eyes to see he already had his trousers on and was adding more wood to the fire. There was an enticing aroma of food surrounding them. She allowed her nose to seek its enjoyment in the cabin's air.

He turned to see her. "Matt reminded me why we were up here. I mean besides this." He waved towards the bed. "I wanted to show you my most favorite place on the ranch, somewhere that means the most to me. To share, I guess."

"It was a beautiful trail as far as I could tell before the snow. The place where we stopped to rest and eat had spectacular views. I can see how it would be a favorite."

He stirred the pot slowly, looking up as if remembering another time. "I was very young when my father decided I was old enough to come up here for the first time. We always had the herds up here for the summer. Plenty of grass and water. The Whitewater River comes through here. In the spring, it's roaring so loud you can hear it from inside. This time of year, it's quieter, especially if there hasn't been any rain. You can always depend on it flowing since the mountains always get snow, and snow eventually melts."

She watched the expression in his eyes, the smile playing around his lips, and realized he could be reading the alphabet, and she would sit here entranced by his very voice. Did it happen that quickly? Had she fallen in love with her husband so easily?

"Come on, honey, the stew's done, and the sun's been out for a few hours. All signs of snow clouds are gone. We still have time today to enjoy the high lands." He placed two filled pie pans on the table along with some corn bread.

She nodded and hesitantly climbed out from the furs. The room felt warm as she found her camisole and pulled it on followed by her dress. All her things were made so she could dress herself, and she was glad of the distraction, so she wouldn't need to face her husband. Not because she was embarrassed any longer, but because she wasn't.

She was used to his eyes caressing her when he caught sight of her bare skin. She was used to his touch and his scent. She missed his hands on her body, anywhere on her body, and wanted to touch him in the same fearless manner. She knew he wouldn't turn her down or worse, merely tolerate her. She was already accepting being his companion, his lover, and his wife. It felt so right she couldn't understand why this hadn't happened sooner.

"This smells wonderful. Was all that talk about not being able to cook simply to make me feel needed?"

His eyes met hers. "You are needed. Much more than you know and not just for your cooking. I see the way all the boys turn to you for advice, how they seek your approval for any little thing they can drag out and brag about their day. Of how conversations occur around the supper table, and I find out things I never knew, and they're telling an almost stranger."

"Is that how you see me? As a stranger, a competitor for your brothers' time?"

"No, I could never give them what you give them. Just being a woman gives you credentials I don't have. I know Andy's been going to church for some reason other than to drive the wagon. Simon can do that if you needed him to."

She sat down at the table and smiled over the aroma of her first real meal in days. She said a quick grace and took up the spoon. Looking over at the pile of furs, she asked, "What kind of stew is this?"

"Beef, from our own herd. I had one butchered since we still had ice and were low on provisions. It should taste pretty good."

"It smells delicious." The first sip proved her husband's cooking skills—he had some.

"Like I said, I had other plans than making love, although that one ended uppermost in my mind."

She felt the warmth travel from her neck to her cheeks to the top of her head. Would she ever get so blasé about the intimacies of marriage that she too could speak about it so calmly? Or would she blush rosily to let everyone know her very intimate thoughts?

"This is very good."

He glanced up from his bowl. "I can cook some, but I'd rather be out with the work. It takes time to get in supplies and make a meal. You do it so well, why would I want to take the job back?"

"So, it's cupboard love?" She teased, then thought better of it and paid attention to her meal rather than see the denial of any emotion in her husband's eyes.

"Right after this, I think we should take advantage of the sunshine and hike to the river. We built a little way from the bank, so if it flooded, the cabin would be safe. There's someplace I want you to see before we leave."

Her heart sank. She was just beginning to enjoy the freedom to look at him without worrying what she was giving away. She liked hearing him speak to her without thinking what others would say. She liked having the freedom to take his hand and know he would hold hers as well.

They dressed as warmly as they could, but he was right. The clear sky and the sun's rays had warmed the earth. Small melting piles where snow had blown up against boulders were all that proved the snowstorm hadn't been her imagination. The bare earth was wet, but their walk was unimpeded as they followed a worn track.

The river was impressive even at this time of year. She could imagine cattle grazing in small groups below them and see where the bank was beaten down as they came for water. He took her hand and walked upriver to a bend where the rushing water sounded louder. The air was crisp, the breeze free of odors. She liked the mossy smell of spring and the pungent smell of dried leaves in the fall, but this was clear clean air. It carried no scent of season with it. Fresh was one word that kept coming to mind.

"I think the waterfall cleans the air," he said as if reading her mind. "I would come up here to fish and fall asleep listening to this sound. Not just the rapids, but the spray from the water cascading over the boulders does something to the air."

She turned to him. "I was thinking the same thing. As if the air is freshened, renewed."

They continued to hold hands.

"My big plans had you and me skinny-dipping here. I had it all planned out. How I would coax you to take off your shoes and stockings so we could wade, and then remove your dress so the hem didn't get wet."

"In this scenario, did I ever put up a fuss and say the river was too dang cold?"

He laughed, then grinned. "Not in my dreams, although by the time I got to this point I was so hard for you I wasn't thinking clearly at all."

She chuckled at his honesty even if it was somewhat embarrassing. Again, letting her scruples, shyness, or whatever get in her way of being at ease with this man. "I might have gone swimming with you naked if the water was warm. I think I've come a long way…"

He swung her in front of him, pulling her into his arms. "Further than I ever dreamt." He nuzzled into her neck, tickling her again. "I'm glad I could make this trip with you. Before, we only came here to bring the cattle up and to drive them back down. I like them closer to the ranch, especially the ones due to birth in case there's a late snowstorm up here. As you've seen, the weather here is unpredictable and harsh at times."

She stepped back to gaze around them, taking in the beauty and majesty of it all. "But I still see why it's your favorite spot. The views are lovely, and I feel on top of the world even though I know there is much more mountain above."

"Come here, and let me help you keep warm." He

wrapped his arms around her and hugged her to him as they gazed over the vista in front of them. She enjoyed the view but enjoyed his holding her more. She wished this could be the way they always were.

However, there was Simon who needed a mother, the twins who needed a representative, Andrew who needed help wooing the minister's daughter, Bartholomew who needed help being heard, and Matthew who needed to feel free enough to live his own life.

If she felt the pressure of trying to do the right thing for each family member, how much harder was it for Luke? From a very young age, he had shouldered the responsibility of his family's livelihood as well as their safety and happiness. She knew he felt as if he failed his mother, but the woman actually had given him a compliment. She went to her maker knowing her children were well cared for as well as loved, but how could Lorelei prove it to him.

He had borne the burden for so long he even felt guilty taking this time for himself. All she could do was support his decisions or change them when she could so the whole Foster family could grow and eventually lead the lives they wanted.

The cold of dusk drove them back to the warmth of the cabin, but their closeness was sealed by their time together. They finished the stew and cleaned up afterward.

"This is the last night here I'm afraid, honey. I don't dare stay longer. Matt will never say he needs help, but his heart isn't in the ranch. Never has been."

She snuggled down into the furs. This wasn't a time to bring up Matthew's dreams.

After tossing more wood on the fire, he shrugged out of his trousers and lifted the blankets to join her. This time, she watched openly, forcing her shyness out of their marriage bed. She noticed he didn't appear as she thought he would.

As he laid back with his arm behind his head as a pillow, she needed answers. "Luke, something's different about you tonight."

"You're curious about me?"

She nodded but knew he could see her as well as she could see him in the stove's firelight.

"Then touch me. I've done most of the work around here so far. Now it's your turn. Touch me." His words were serious, yet he had a dimpled grin on his face.

She bolstered her courage and reached toward his crotch, finding the thick mat of fur. "Oh, you're soft and small and...oh-h-h, I think I understand. You change. You're growing even as I hold you."

He hissed slowly.

She stopped her tentative explorations. "Does it hurt?"

"No, it feels so good I can't explain how good. It feels a whole bunch good."

She smiled and kissed his mouth as she felt him tense and flex under her hands. "So, you like me touching you like this? And this?"

Each question earned her a groan, but he didn't raise his hand to stop her or help her. She continued her study of his body, furthering her knowledge of him and what he seemed to like most. The mapping of his body had done things to her as well. She was no longer content to have him guide their lovemaking or set the pace.

She swung her leg over him and impaled herself on his rigid phallus, which was now more than cooperative. "You can participate or just lie there and take it like a man."

"I'm letting you run things this time, but remember I have the upper hand."

"You think so, do you? We'll talk about that when I'm done with you." Her smile was wide as she set the pace and drove him to a frenzy before she finally gave him relief.

Snuggling onto his chest, she tugged a fur in place over them both. "Did I do everything right? Are there suggestions for next time?"

"No, just knowing there is going to be a next time is more than I need to know to keep going. Mrs. Foster, you do surprise me more and more every day. You are more than I ever thought of having for a wife." He kissed her head as he breathed in deeply and settled for the night. "How did I ever get so lucky?"

"I think it had something to do with an unexpected fire and an expected librarian." A smile for that day she thought had ruined her life. Instead, it had made her the happiest of women.

CHAPTER NINE

"Are you sure, Dorothy? I think it's about time someone did something about Helen being out there all alone. Well, not exactly alone, but someone needs to help."

"Lorelei, I heard this from a customer who drives past the farm, and then I saw Toby and verified the facts. That last windstorm brought down the building they housed the cow in and killed it. There was more damage, but that was the worst part. She sold me butter sometimes to pay for groceries, and I know having the milk for the children was a necessity."

The two women spoke quietly but still raised their heads at the sound of the door chime.

Sarah Ann, the minister's daughter who had become one of Lorelei's confidants, hurried over to the two older friends. "What are you huddled here discussing? You both looked like you got caught with your hands in the cookie jar."

Dorothy welcomed the younger woman. "The Wilkes' farm lost its barn and their cow with it. We were trying to figure out a way to help. Helen doesn't take charity."

"Helping a neighbor isn't charity. We've done barn raisings in the past after all," Sarah Ann said. "Why don't we simply go out there and do it ourselves?"

Lorelei was so surprised at the idea she sputtered,

"I, I, I think that's a great idea. I can get a pair of the twins' overalls and work gloves, probably some supplies and tools from the barn."

"Bring me a pair of those overalls," Sarah Ann instructed. "This would be a good time to take the dress and skirts I have set aside to Hannah. I can bring a hammer and saw, but Papa doesn't have many tools. We hire things done mostly."

Lorelei had to ask, "What's this about a dress?"

Calm little Sarah Ann almost stamped her foot she was so angry. "Last spring Hannah was shamed in front of the whole school by the teacher, Mr. Meeks. He said she should stop dressing like a ruffian and start dressing like a girl. She ran out and hasn't been back. All she has are her father's shirts and overalls to wear. Toby wears her hand-me-downs. Us showing up wearing them should give a boost to her self-esteem. If grown women can wear them, then she can as well. I have a dress for her to wear to school."

Lorelei added, "I have a couple of things, also. Perhaps if we leave them with her and not say too much, she'll accept them. I take it she's as proud as her mother?"

"She's been punished at school for fighting—with the boys." Dorothy rolled her eyes as she said this last bit.

"Then it's settled. We'll get what we need and go out there to help. Now when should we go?" Lorelei was mentally checking her commitments for the week but found nothing she couldn't change for another day.

"The sooner the better I say," Dorothy added.

Lorelei nodded in agreement. "Tomorrow morning. I'll tell the boys I'm going to a quilting bee and won't be home until it's done. They have no idea how long that means, and I'll leave them a meal."

Lorelei saw Helen come out the back door and lift her hand to shade her eyes from the sun. She proudly sat astride Buttercup wearing the denim overalls. The only person they saw on the way was the doctor coming back from a house call, but he tipped his hat. Didn't seem interested in the way she and Sarah Ann were dressed.

Now they faced Helen, who they didn't wish to offend, but knew she needed help. The woman was practically skin and bones trying to keep the farm chores up as well as care for a family.

Lorelei decided on the attack plan as she slid to the ground. "I don't want to hear a lot about you not needing help or that you can get it done as soon as you finish something else. We are your friends, and as such, we have the right, no, the duty, to help when things like this happen. Consider it our gift to you—one friend to another."

She wasn't sure if it was her bravado or if Helen felt overwhelmed, but the haggard-appearing mother merely waved her hand at the tumbled-down building. "I tried all yesterday to pull it into position, but it just kept leaning back over. The beams are split at the ground, and I can't shore it up at the same time I get it pulled into shape."

"That's why we're here. I brought some tools, but this looks worse than I thought. I can go back to town once we know what all we'll be needing." Lorelei took note of the missing shingles and broken window in the stable.

Dorothy dismounted and got out a wrapped parcel. She was wearing a worn work dress with a few paint smears on the skirt. "May be best to clear out the broken boards and see what's salvageable. Helen, don't let us interrupt your day." Her no-nonsense way sent Helen back into the house while Sarah Ann, looking darling in Paul's hand-me-downs, waited for orders.

The three women went to the pile of rubble and began pulling the loose boards out. Lorelei took charge. "Sarah Ann, can you pound out the nails and place them in a pile over there. We can reuse the nails too if they're not too bent. Dorothy, maybe you and I can jerry-rig this pulley Helen has hooked to the roof and pull it back in place using that tree branch."

The two women tried but found there wasn't any way they could support the walls so began dismantling them and making a pile of boards good enough to reuse. The sound of horses and wagon approaching the farm made Lorelei and Dorothy raise their heads with questioning expressions.

Lorelei's stomach dropped when she recognized the driver as Luke with Andrew to his side and the one on horseback as Matthew. She felt guilty for not being completely honest about where she was going that morning, but not in what she was trying to do. She motioned Dorothy to keep working while she walked across the yard to meet her family members.

"Luke, were you looking for me?"

Her husband gazed into her eyes but stated baldly. "Nope. Knew where you were and what you were up to. We stopped by to get what we thought might be needed for the job before following."

"I, ah, didn't think we needed help." She watched

as her brother-in-law dismounted and put on a work belt holding hammers, chisels, and other tools she didn't recognize. "You're here to help?"

Matthew walked toward the rubble. "That's what neighbors do, isn't it?"

Luke got down and opened the wagon's gate. "I'll leave everything here for now. The supper you left for the boys at home is in that basket, so Mrs. Wilkes won't need to worry about feeding us. I put beans on to soak for them."

"Oh, Luke, you didn't need to do that. We brought a lunch."

"But not enough to feed three hungry men. The boys will make do with beans and ham. There's plenty of bread, or Bart can make biscuits. Now let's get to work so we can be done by dusk."

She watched as he strode away. Her heart swelled with pride that he would come all this way to help a woman whom he doesn't know. She saw Helen at the back door and went to explain.

"The men felt they had a day to spare, so they followed us to help. Brought a meal for us all. As long as I'm confessing, Sarah Ann and I brought a couple of things that will fit Hannah. Clothes for her to wear to school. A girl needs education. We can't always depend on a husband to support us."

The woman's sad eyes stared into hers. "It's hard to admit I can't do it all. I mean, with my husband, I had a chance on this farm, but it needed work when we bought it. Now, it's gone downhill the past few years." She wiped her hands on her apron deciding whether to accept the bundle held out to her. "Hannah will be pleased to accept these. She looks up to Sarah Ann.

Always says she's dressed right pretty."

Lorelei said, "I noticed her feet were about the same size as mine, so I added a pair of shoes. If they don't fit, you let me know. I figured that was why she hasn't been to church."

"She grew like a weed this past year, and overalls were the only thing that could keep up with her, you know? Just let the straps out a little and they fit, but feet are different, feet can't be contained."

Patting Helen's hand, Lorelei said, "I better get back so the others don't think I'm standing here gossiping."

She walked back to Dorothy who was helping pile boards alongside Sarah Ann. The men were using the pulley, but their strength made the job look easy. Luke and Matthew held the rope while Andrew pounded boards in place.

Luke called over, "There are fence posts in the wagon. Maybe a couple of you can work on getting the paddock fixed well enough to hold animals."

Lorelei nodded, and Dorothy went with her, bringing the wagon closer so the wood was within easy reach.

Just after lunch, which Helen served on the table she brought outside and benches made of boards from the wagon with chairs supporting each end, more surprises arrived. Helen shooed them off as she began the cleanup when Simon and Toby showed up.

This time Helen had trouble hiding her tears. Behind Toby was a milk cow, her bell around her neck clanging with each step. Behind Simon was a heifer from the Foster's own herd.

"She's gonna have a baby, Ma. Not the cow, the

other one, she's gonna have a calf come spring."

Helen wiped her eyes with the end of her apron. "Tie them up somewhere, and come get some vittles. I was just about to clear this all away."

Now Lorelei understood why she and Dorothy were sent to fix the fence on the enclosure. It needed to be ready for these two animals. The children wouldn't be without their milk. Over an hour later, she made sure the last of the posts were secure and moved the wagon team into the shade.

Taking off her work gloves, Dorothy motioned over to where Andrew was helping Sarah Ann. "Those two getting to be a couple? Her daddy approve?"

"I'm not sure. She seems to fancy him, and he's been going to church each Sunday but always sits with Simon and me. Of course, if and when they sit together in her daddy's church, then we'll probably be hearing of a date set." Lorelei felt that time may be coming soon.

"They make a cute couple. But then, any of the Foster boys would make a cute half of any couple." Dorothy pulled her gloves back on and called over to the men. "I saw shingles in the back of the wagon. You want those over by you now?"

Matthew smiled over, "Yep, we're ready for them, but I'll take a couple bundles for the house. Looks like it lost some during the storm as well." He strode past, lifted a bundle onto his shoulder, and easily carried it over to the farmhouse.

By the time Lorelei was brushing the dust and hay off her legs, the stable was up, and the animal stalls readied, a full sack of feed was in the bin, and the roof reshingled. She almost laughed aloud at her optimistic plans to repair the damaged building. How Helen could maintain this farm as well as she had on her own was amazing.

They were leaving the woman much better off than when they arrived that morning and that had been the main goal. The fact they had the Foster men to thank for most of it was not going to diminish her feeling of accomplishment. The farmhouse had almost a whole new roof, and the stable was rain tight. The fencing was repaired or replaced and would hold the animals when they were let outside. It would give the widow time to work on other jobs that still needed to be done while the weather was good.

She accepted Helen's thanks and took the cleaned dishes placing them into the wagon. Luke was closing the gate as he said gruffly, "Andy's gonna see Miss Sarah Ann home on your horse, so you're to ride with me."

During the hours when the men were working, she had taken his orders, but now, for some reason, it riled her. She didn't want to put a strain on the ride home or allow Helen to think she caused a breach between her friends, so she climbed up to the wagon bench and sat down, feeling strange at not having any skirts to shuffle around. The ease of wearing trousers surprised her, and she wished she could do so every day.

Luke climbed up somberly, again refusing to meet her gaze. She was beginning to feel the need to have a talk with her husband, even if it turned into an outright war. She felt his antagonism from the moment he pulled into the yard with the wagon.

However, if he didn't want to help today, he should have stayed home. She didn't ask him to come.

Probably, Sarah Ann had said something to Andrew. Her brother-in-law would be the type to take a day to help, even if it was only to be close to his favorite girl. He had worked mostly by Sarah Ann's side when he could but went willingly to help the other men when he was called to do so.

Andrew's willingness to help only pointed out how belligerent Luke was acting. He worked just as hard, but there was something about how he looked at her the few times she caught him taking a break from nailing shingles or fitting doors. Like he wanted to be elsewhere. He seemed to smolder with resentment.

They rode in silence, her husband's bad temper causing all joy from the day to leave her. Now she had another reason to be angry at his behavior. She rubbed the blisters on her right hand caused from pulling and pounding so many nails that day. With each painful reminder, she became angrier with the man who now bore the brunt of everything that had gone wrong that morning before the men showed up.

She should have realized they needed a wagon to haul wood and shingles. She should have realized that three women, even four if they allowed Helen to help, couldn't lift a barn back in place. She should be thanking Luke for allowing his brothers to help.

"Luke," she said, quietly placing her hand on his knee.

He tensed under her touch and with a hard gaze stared at her hand. She withdrew it and tried to reach an amicable rapport again. "Luke, I wasn't trying to hide anything from you. I know how busy you and the boys are, so I made the arrangements myself. I may not have planned things very well, but I didn't mean for it to be a secret from you or anything."

"I know."

Well, at least he warmed enough to speak so she continued. "So, you'll stop being mad at me?"

His eyes flashed toward her with his brows drawn down. "I'm not mad. Why do you say that?"

"This is the first you've looked directly at me all day, and if I come within your sight, you're all furious frown. I said I was sorry."

He shook his head but turned back to watching the road, the fierce expression back on his face.

"Stop the wagon! Stop, or I'll jump." She was mad. She could be furious and headstrong, too. "Are those our haystacks?"

He nodded but remained looking at the horse's back ends.

"Then I'm cutting across them to reach the ranch house. I don't need to stay with you and be condemned for being a good neighbor." She jumped down and thanked the fates she was wearing britches that made it so easy to do so. She strode toward the split-rail fence when she heard him land on the hard-baked earth, and then his legs cutting through the tall dry grass alongside the road behind her.

He spun her around, grabbing her wrists, holding them between them. "What are you rambling on about? I'm not mad at you about helping Helen or being a good neighbor." He looked around as if someone may overhear him. "I'm wound up tight as a knot over seeing you in those overalls. My neither region has been aroused since seein' you as I pulled into the yard. Matt's been enjoying my misery all afternoon, laughing every time he caught me watching your, um, you as you worked."

Feeling her face flush red, she stammered, "O-oh, I'm sorry, I…"

"Doesn't matter. Sooner we're home, sooner I can get away from you. I'll calm down or maybe take a swim in the horse tank. That should do it."

This brought up another point that had rankled between them. "Maybe it wasn't such a good idea to go back to sleeping in the babies' room when we returned from the cabin. I thought after our trip we would share a bed."

"Matt's doing again. He teased I should leave you some sense of privacy. After him saying those things about me not knowing you didn't know how to ride and askin' if you could still walk the next day…Even hinted I might scare you off if I kept, um, after you."

She glanced both directions down the road. "Do you think you can make it over the fence and behind one of those hay mounds in your delicate condition?"

His scowl became raised highbrows, and a grin replaced the pouty frown. "I can if you can." He swung her into his arms and took the few strides setting her on the other side of the low fence. Placing a hand on the top rail, he jumped over and found himself at her mercy.

She began to fumble with his trouser buttons, intent on getting them down before worrying about her own state of overdress. He was working at unhooking the buttons from the shoulder straps of her overalls and working his way out of his trousers while pushing her onto her back into the hay.

Shimmying out of the garment's legs, she felt the familiar touch of her husband's skin. She met his lips as they continued to cover her face with kisses. He pushed up her shirt and camisole, claiming her breasts as his own. She pushed up toward him, reveling in his enjoyment of having her body in his hands.

She gave free rein to her hands to touch and her mouth to taste and her body to feel as he entered her possessively. He held her buttocks, thrusting vigorously until they both exploded internally, their bodies stiffening and their breathing ragged.

He stayed on top of her until she moved to give her arms relief. He slid to her side but stayed half on top of her nuzzling her neck. "I don't know how I kept my hands off you. Every time I saw your cute little fanny, I turned to lust. Had trouble getting off the wagon when I first got there."

"Sarah Ann was wearing overalls, too. You talked to her at supper. You smiled at her. Now you're telling me you didn't lust after her?"

"I don't feel the same around her. Andy probably felt like me, though. Hard on him since I'm pretty sure he isn't doing what we just did."

"Is that the Foster brothers' oath not to poach on each other's preserves?"

He gazed down at her. "Matt and his big mouth. I had no thought for anyone but you, and they were the same thoughts over and over. How do I get back to where we were at the cabin? I felt we were really a couple there. Is it having all the boys around us, do you think?"

She twirled her fingers through his hair, his hat on the other side of the fence where it fell. "We are a couple, and I think everyone accepts that fact—but us. You once said everyone thought we were already sleeping together. Perhaps we should go on that premise and live as man and wife in a midst of a large family."

He kissed her then kissed her again. "I agree, Mrs. Foster. From tonight on, we share a bed and all that means." He kissed her breasts, then pulled her shirt back into place before pulling his trousers up which never got completely off.

She smiled thinking of how quickly they decided to make love. Evidently, lust affected both sexes. She pulled the straps over her shoulder, and by the time she felt presentable, Luke was redressed as well. He took her hand and walked to the fence. Then he lifted her over and set her feet on the ground before following her. He leaned down as they passed to retrieve his hat.

When they reached the wagon, he grinned cheekily, "Do you need help up, or can I just watch you from here?"

She looked back at him, and wagging her backend like a happy dog, climbed onto the bench seat.

CHAPTER TEN

He saw his younger brother as soon as they pulled the horses to a stop in the yard. "Put the wagon away for me, will you, Paul?"

Chagrin filled his mind as he remembered what he had just had the boldness to do, what his wife actually instigated, and how much he wanted to repeat the afternoon. Making love outside. Leaving the team standing on the road and tearing one another's clothes off to make love where ever they found themselves. If he had thought that was a possibility this afternoon, he wouldn't have been able to control his body at all. That would have been all he thought of, along with how sexy his wife was wearing his brother's hand-me-downs.

Matt was inside cooking at the stove. "What kept you two so long?" As he glanced up catching Lori ducking her red face and heading for the stairs, he finished with, "Oh-h-h-h."

Luke walked closer to him. "Don't say another word about anything, or I swear I'll…"

"Then don't come home with straw in your hair, big brother. Sets a bad example and makes some of us downright jealous."

"I was working on a barn." But couldn't help the grin he knew was pasted on his face.

He swatted Matt's hand away as he tried to pull the offending piece of hay out of his hair. Pouring some hot water into a bucket, he took it upstairs with him. No need for a cooling-off swim this evening. His mind was on whether or not he would be able to talk Lori into letting him watch her wash or letting him wash her as they explored their new relationship.

His body responded to either scenario as he climbed the stairs two at a time.

The next morning, Lorelei had never been happier or more content. Luke nuzzled into her neck after making love to her. "I've got to finish cutting that hay before it rains. Can I trust you to dress in your own clothes today and stay on the ranch?"

"I plan on wearing my own clothes all day, but I'm afraid to say I have a meeting with the school board and possibly the schoolmaster in town. Several of us parents are not satisfied with the methods of teaching Mr. Meeks uses."

"Parents, huh?" He swung his bare feet out of bed followed by his bare buttocks. She watched as he pulled on his trousers and socks. He searched through the bureau drawers for a shirt. She admired the ripple of muscles across his back as he finally made his selection and pulled the cavalry-styled shirt over his head.

He paused to look at her. "Please don't get arrested. I don't plan to be back until almost dark, and I won't let them keep you from me overnight."

"Hm-m-m-m-m, worried you won't sleep well?"

"I know I won't sleep well." He rubbed his hand over his stubble. "I think I'll skip shaving since I shaved last night." He gave her one of his salacious grins and headed for the stairs.

"Tell everyone I'll be right down to make

117

breakfast. Flapjacks, eggs, and sausage. If you see Simon, have him bring in the eggs first thing."

Sitting in the audience of parents, able to break away from work long enough to attend the afternoon school board meeting, Lorelei nodded to many whom she already knew. She hadn't been in Whitewater Rapids very long, and yet, it felt like home, more like home than the two-storied house she and her father lived in for years in Cincinnati ever had.

There she knew few of their neighbors because she spent her days working alongside her father once she graduated. Here she was accepted as Luke's wife and guardian of his younger brothers just as he was. She smiled in welcome as Dorothy sat next to her, and the chairman began to call the meeting to order.

By the end of the meeting, she was so irate she could hardly hold herself in the chair.

Dorothy leaned over as the school board members quickly filed out of the room. "They aren't going to say anything to the man. My girls are afraid to return this fall. I may have to teach them myself."

The common thoughts and complaints were that the schoolmaster was too brutal in his punishments of students, especially the older boys. Every parent agreed children needed firm control and punishments for disobeying rules to learn, and classes needed to maintain discipline. The problem was the definition of how that punishment should be meted out and how often.

Lorelei felt children who never had a disciplinary problem were afraid of the teacher. She felt she had no place in the complaints because other than hearsay, she had nothing to prove her brothers had been unfairly chastised. She only knew they were good boys and not prone to disobeying rules. In fact, they had never complained about doing the hard work she knew they did every day. In addition, Simon wasn't a boy to ignore any adult's request or order.

She wanted to meet Mr. Meeks, the paragon the board supported without reservation. She could not believe any man dedicated to educating children believed in such harsh corporal punishment as to leave marks on children's legs from riding crops or bruises from wooden rulers. What could an eight-year-old do to warrant such brutality?

She waved to Helen, but that woman had two young children waiting for her, so Lorelei walked from the community building past the once burned-out library. There had been some work done, the burned bricks and timbers removed, and she could imagine what it will appear as it is rebuilt. She continued and found herself outside the school at the far end of the main street.

There was a motion by the door, a string-thin man poked his head out, then pulled it back in like a frightened turtle. That must be Mr. Meeks she thought as she picked up the edge of her skirts and marched up the path to the steps leading to the white building.

She did not knock. After all, it was a public building, and her husband paid a goodly amount to run the school. "Mr. Meeks? Sir, I would like to speak with you, if I may."

The man she saw dodge into the door stood by the desk at the front of the room. There were several rows of benches lined up in front of him now holding chalkboards and readers.

"May I help you with something, Mrs…?" the young man asked politely.

He was surprisingly young. Younger than she was, and she began to rethink the problem she thought she had.

"Mr. Meeks, I am newly married to Luke Foster. I believe his brothers were students here last year but left early."

She saw him blush, but he remained ramrod straight. "I remember the twins. They decided they no longer needed to attend school. I am not paid to enforce truancy. Besides, they told me they were old enough to make their own decisions."

"I understood they were good students and attended regularly as did Simon. Can you shed light on what went wrong?" She wanted to understand this young man and get her brothers into the school again.

"Simon began running with a bad sort, a boy with no parental guidance, it seems. Toby began by being insubordinate and rude. He refused my orders, and I told him as long as he was a distraction to the others, he could not return to the classroom."

He sounded so smug and sanctimonious Lorelei lost her pleasant demeanor. "Was that before or after you reprimanded his sister, Hannah, for not being properly dressed? Telling her she was a distraction in her overalls and bare feet? Making a young girl feel ashamed for being out in public when her only crime was being poor."

This time, there was no doubt as to his embarrassment. The thin blond hair barely covering the top of his head did nothing to hide the red glow. "After all, people will think she's no better than she should be with a mother like hers. I, ah, I thought it best to tell her she should be wearing dresses and shoes and socks."

"Don't you think she would if she had them? You must know her father died years ago, and all she has to wear are his clothes. There just isn't money to buy material to make dresses for a growing girl. You must make allowances for such children since poverty is present in any community. Making them a laughing point and humiliating them in front of their peers is cruel and helps no one. A child who needs schooling the most is ostracized, and you lose the good opinion of the rest of your class for being a bully."

"I'm the bully? Those two ruffians you call brothers are the real bullies. They threatened me with physical abuse."

"Peter and Paul? When? What did they say?"

He hesitated and glanced away.

"This was after the set-down with Hannah? They didn't like how you treated their classmate?" She could see the two approach this man and tell him where he went wrong. "But they didn't touch you, did they? It was all sort of man to man?"

"I am the schoolmaster. They have no right to speak to me like that."

"Well, as the future member of the school board—I do. I will have all the students back in this classroom come fall or know the reason why. I will make sure everyone understands your position as being in command of this classroom. I will make sure my brothers give you the respect your position deserves."

The man in front of her seemed to preen in her apparent approval of his actions.

"I will also monitor your behavior towards these students. In particular, the male students and the children of the woman you evidently feel it is beneath you to educate. You are paid by the community and as such will treat all students equally as you will their parents. If you do not agree, then there is time for Whitewater Rapids to find another teacher. I will fill in until that schoolmaster can be found. Do I make myself clear?"

He nodded, his eyes wide and his chin trembling.

"If there are any problems with any of my brothers merely pen me a note and the situation will be dealt with immediately. If you have students in need, clothing, food, anything that interferes with their education, please let myself or the minister, who is head of the school board, know. We will make sure the shortage is addressed."

The man seemed to have shrunk and his head lower than when she first entered the schoolroom.

"It was a pleasure to make your acquaintance, Mr. Meeks, and I look forward to working with you in the coming school year. Is there anything else that needs to be addressed?"

"N-no, Ma'am, ah, Mrs. Foster. It will be a pleasure to teach your brothers again."

She nodded as she turned and left. What the man lacked in sincerity, he made up for in healthful fear. She knew she had a wide smile on her face all the way back to the wagon.

Luke stretched and savored the feel of clean sheets beneath his naked body. His eyes snapped open when his hand did not encounter his wife. The other side of the bed was empty. He felt his mouth turn down. Lori always stayed in bed next to him until he got up for the day. Maybe she needed the privy.

She still wasn't back by the time he was ready for the day, but he could smell the odor of cooking as soon as the bedroom door opened. The tightness in his stomach lessened. Even after these weeks of being together, he didn't feel secure. She could still leave when the novelty of their relationship waned. He dreaded the moment and at the same time held his emotions in check so when it happened, he would be able to give strength to the younger boys.

Lori was standing in front of the stove as he entered the parlor. He felt the breath he was holding leave his lungs. He walked up behind her and kissed the nape of her neck. A show of affection he had never done outside their bedroom. "I missed having you in bed with me when I woke up."

She sidestepped him and nervously fumbled with a spatula before flipping a piece of fried bread. "I, ah, nature called. I thought as long as I was awake, I may as well begin breakfast."

The boys' feet thundered down the stairs. "Simon, sit down and eat now. You can get the eggs later."

His youngest brother plopped into his chair at the table and the others followed suit. Lori set the platter of ham and eggs along with another of fried bread. "Come sit down, Lori, you can eat with us."

He couldn't read her expression. She appeared to hide her gaze from him, her conversation much less chatty as the others talked across the table to one another.

"Lori, you're not eating. Should we all worry you

poisoned the food?" he teased but received no smile in return.

"I guess I had too many tastes as I cooked. I'll eat again later." Standing, she began gathering the empty plates and took them to the sink. "I'm going into town, but I don't need anyone to take me. Simon showed me how to drive the team, and I can handle them now."

Luke glanced to his young brother for confirmation. Simon, his mouth full, mumbled, "She can do it. I gave her the reins, and she's driven the wagon full and empty. She can do it."

"I don't care how capable she is, I'll take her in." Luke decided he wanted to stay close to his wife. Since school began, he was needed more in the field, and they hadn't had time to be together. Nighttime was different. She was warm and welcoming and more than he realized a wife was to a husband. They communed with one another, and he hated feeling she was hiding something from him after the closeness they shared at night.

She didn't seem excited to be going to town, not like she usually was, but she did get ready and climbed into the wagon with his help. She remained quiet even after he tried to talk about the schoolmaster and the upcoming town social commemorating the town's founding.

He was racking his brain on what to say to her to have her open up to him about what was bothering her when he felt her slump against his arm. Pulling to a stop, he turned to hold her upright. "Lori, sweetheart, what's wrong? Are you sick? Do you want some water?"

She moaned and let her head drop to her chest. He

shook her to get her eyes to open a slit, but he didn't like the paleness of her skin or the slackness around her mouth. He laid her down on the bench seat, chafing her hand until her eyelids flickered open.

She sat up and placed a hand on her waist before spinning to retch over the side of the wagon. She brushed his hands off her shoulder and remained bent over the side, her hands holding onto the edge of the seat. She finally sat straighter but remained silent.

"Sweetheart, what can I do to help? Should I take you to see the doctor?"

"No! Take me to Helen. She'll know what to do."

Luke reluctantly set the team in motion but held Lori against his side. He couldn't help but worry and wanted the horses to go faster yet knew the extra bouncing and jostling might be too much for her stomach.

They moved through town past the sign proclaiming the white building at the end of town as belonging to Doctor Hatch. He kept looking at the sign, and as they continued, he wished he dared argue with her and took her to the doctor instead of needing to drive another half hour. The sight of the farm looked considerably better since he last visited when he helped put the stable back up. Mrs. Wilkes must have been able to pay for paint since both the house and stable looked refreshed with a coat of whitewash.

As he stopped the wagon once again, he half-hoped the woman wasn't there. Instead, he heard her voice as she emerged from the house.

"Lori, this is a surprise. I thought we were meeting at the end of next week."

Lori seemed to glance away from him once more,

and the pit of his stomach felt tight again. Why did this feel so unsettling? He worried about his marriage and his wife. His life was so tightly wound with Lori's he wasn't sure what he would do if she decided to leave him. After all, their marriage wasn't entered into with the strongest of reasons, and now, she may be looking for a way out. Making herself sick with the worry of how to do that.

The two women huddled with their heads together as he took the horses to the watering trough. As he walked back, they were hugging and laughing. All signs of his sick wife gone and his rosy-cheeked bride back in sight. He felt light-headed and sped up as he heeded the need to be next to her. If her spirits could lift so quickly, her ailment wasn't dangerous and her worry easily put aside. They might have a chance. She might stay with him.

Helen was all smiles. "Luke, you want some tea or coffee? I can whip up either pretty fast."

"Ah, whatever Lori wants is fine by me." After Helen went back into the house, he turned to his wife. He knew his face must have shown his question. "You really feeling better, sweetheart? We can still find the doc if you want."

Incongruously she answered, "This may be the best place to find him."

"Oh, the little ones here need him that often? That's a shame. They look healthy enough. Do you think she needs help with the costs?" He glanced to the back door so their hostess wouldn't catch them talking about her.

Lori slipped her arm into his. "Let's go in and have our visit. Then we can drive back by lunchtime. I had a special supper planned for us." She leaned against him as they walked toward the house.

He shook his head as he thought about all the dire outcomes he feared from his wife's sign of illness and her uncommunicative behavior since he woke. Would he ever understand her? He patted her hand as they climbed the two steps and entered the cooler home.

On the return ride home, Lori asked him to come to a stop again. It was at the same hayfield they made love in weeks earlier. His wife was happier and more relaxed this time as they rode through town and past the doctor's office. He was still feeling good about the trip.

"This reminds me of a pleasant afternoon. Could I talk you into resting against one of the haystacks?" He made the teasing offer.

She blushed and glanced into the field. "I should get back to the ranch house. Maybe later?"

She gave him hope, and that was all he needed at this time. The knowledge she planned to stay and that she planned to remain a wife to him. "Just let me know when. You ready to move on?"

Instead of telling him to keep going, she started talking. He was worried there was something more going on with her so waited and listened.

"I was very worried this morning when I became so ill. I woke up sick, and I needed another's opinion."

He tried not to show his frustration or anger. "I said we should have stopped at the doctor's place. We can get back there right now. I want you seen to."

She covered his hands with her own. "No, I'll be fine. Maybe sick for a few more weeks, but then I should settle down."

"That ain't acceptable to me. I'm taking you to the

127

doc." He reached to lead the team to turn around in the dusty road.

"Luke, I'm going to have a baby. I will be sick most mornings, but it hopefully won't last long. I should be able to do my work and keep up with everything."

It took a moment for the thought to sink in, then his heart began pounding and he grabbed his wife, kissing her before allowing her to sit back onto the seat. "You don't need to work at all. We can do for ourselves. You need to rest and, ah, eat good food, and, ah, I don't know what else. What did Helen say?"

"That I was doing just as I should. That I will be ill most mornings, but it can continue all day. I will be tired and want to nap. She suggests I do that whenever I can. And the rest will progress."

"All that in just a few minutes together? I was so worried about you, honey."

"I'm sorry, but I didn't want you to get excited if I was wrong. I needed Helen to explain I was with child and that I was supposed to feel this way."

"Then I owe her a favor." He lifted her onto his lap and nuzzled her neck, leaving a path of kisses. "I was so frightened you were leaving me. At least thinking of leaving me…"

"Never. I will never leave you, and now we will have the child to think about. You're a wonderful man and will make a wonderful father. After all, you've raised these brothers into independent men. You will be a good father to our children, Luke. That was never one of my worries."

"I'm not worried about that, sweetheart, I'm worried about you. You're not very big, and I know how difficult giving birth is on a woman. I'm not sure I can be as happy or as calm about you having a child, although I never took care for you not to become pregnant."

"I knew what I was doing. I knew this was the outcome of what we were doing, and I wasn't afraid of becoming a mother. It was part of my planned life. Don't lessen my joy by saying you wish now I wasn't having this baby."

"No, I didn't mean that, not at all. I think every man worries about his woman having his child. I have so many feelings going through me right now, but one thing never changes. I want this child, and I want you. Those two things are all that matter to me."

"I won't leave you. This is our child we're talking about. I will not lose our child."

They kissed until the hot, fall sun drove them to continue their trip to their home. His emotions were high, and he wanted to tell everyone he was going to be a father. Wanted to show everyone this woman belonged to him. He knew it was wrong, but it didn't stop him from feeling that way.

CHAPTER ELEVEN

Lorelei hung up the last shirt for the day and looked at the heavily laden rope lines held high by the notched poles. She went back to dump the cooling water and snatch up the empty laundry basket to hang on the porch wall next to the tub.

The odd sound took a moment to register before she pulled her hand back. Too late. The rattler struck her, and she felt the needle-like fangs puncture her skin at the inside of her arm. She swung out, taking the snake with her. It dropped and slithered away, but the damage was done. She couldn't suck the poison out from that position, the only emergency method she could think of to save herself, to save her baby. She needed help and quickly. Running to the dinner bell, she rang it twice before collapsing. The sound of her heart thrummed through her ears. The pain shot up her arm making every vein burn on its way.

Thinking she should tie off her upper arm, she tried to look around for a bandana or strip of cloth. She felt her eyes flutter close, her breathing harsh in the darkness. Unable to stay awake, she was weak and groggy. Dragging in deep breaths, she prayed someone heard the bell.

Luke raised his head after cutting the grubworm out of the calf's hide and pouring boric acid on the open wound. He listened intently, sure he heard the bell sound out through the cool fall air. But Lori knew to ring several times if she wanted someone to come home. What if she were ill and couldn't ring more than once or someone prevented her from ringing it.

Dropping his probe, he jumped onto his startled horse. Kicking it into motion, it reared and turned toward the ranch at breakneck speed. His mind was on his wife and their child. What if Lori had fallen and was in pain. What if she was losing the baby? It was early days yet, but he knew such things could happen.

His breathing kept pace with the horse's hooves. He felt the sweat of exertion and worry trickle down his neck and soak his shirt. Ignoring the discomfort, he saw the ranch come into view. Saw the lines full of clean wash blowing in the breeze and pile of clothes on the back steps waiting to be washed. No unfamiliar horses to indicate intruders. Nothing to alarm him.

He strained to see his wife, see her smiling face welcoming him home, but he didn't see that either. The pile of clothes turned into the slumped body of his wife leaning against the back door. Jumping off his horse before it came to a stop, he dropped the reins rushing to her side.

"Lori, honey, come on wake up. Lori."

He felt for a pulse and listened to her labored breathing. It reminded him of his mother's just before she died. Drawing in air noisily. Her body not satisfied with the amount it received. He searched for any sign of trauma but found nothing. He stood and rang the bell vigorously so others could come and go for the doctor.

Scooping her up, he used her foot to open the door and carried her to their room.

He called her name, hoping the jostling and movement would wake her. He was hoping this was simply a faint due to her expecting their child. Nothing more than woman problems. Something that would disappear soon.

He laid a wet cloth on her forehead hoping it was just a little heat stroke from working with the hot laundry water. Anything he could blame easily, anything that wouldn't take her life.

Matt was running through the house yelling, "Luke, what happened? Where's Lori? I found your horse wandering to the paddock."

"Get the doc. I don't know what's happened. Tell him she's a couple months with child, but there's no blood. I can't wake her." He heard the sound of boots go back out the door, and he turned worried eyes to his wife.

She looked so alone there, pale and her breathing still labored and harsh sounding. He untied the apron and pulled it from her body then to the skirt's waist. The doctor would want to examine her to find out what was wrong. As he pulled off her blouse, he saw the drops of blood above the inside of her elbow.

He held her arm gently and examined the double needle-thin holes. His heartbeats went into triple-time, his breathing fast and shallow and the sweat beaded on his forehead. All the symptoms he saw in his wife. A rattler had bitten her. He recognized the marks immediately.

He sucked at the sight of the bite and spit, but he knew he only tasted her. The venom was already coursing through her body. Did that mean it was coursing through the baby's as well? He hated thinking of the damage it could do to either of the most precious people in his world.

Kneeling on the floor, he laid his head on his wife and their child. He hadn't felt like this even when he held his father's limp form in his arms, not even when he heard the last struggling breath from his mother. How would he survive, and did he want to without her, without them?

"Don't leave me, Lori. Please don't leave me. I love you too much to want to go on without you. Don't leave me alone."

He did something he hadn't done since his father's death. He prayed. "Please don't take her. I know I don't have the right to ask, but please don't take her. She's so good and always helps others. I should go instead."

He wasn't sure how long he stayed that way making promises and bargains, but nothing worked. His pleas were turned down, and his wife remained pale and clammy to his touch. He thought that might be better than a fever. After all, it would be with a heifer. A fever meant complications, a putrid of the blood, certain death.

He heard the doctor's voice, and then Matt's, as he ushered the older man up the stairs. Luke hadn't had much to do with this doctor since the boys were relatively healthy and so far, hadn't needed bones set.

"Doc, I found where a rattler got her. See right here and I sucked at it, but I didn't taste anything. Shouldn't I have tasted something bitter or…?"

"Hang on, son. Let me get a look at her."

Luke stopped talking and stepped back. He saw Matt outside the door appearing worried. "Tell the others to look for a snake near the backyard. Maybe trying to find a warm place under the porch."

"What should I tell them about Lori?"

He looked to his wife. "Tell them she's alive, and that's all we have right now. She's been unconscious since I found her outside."

Matt nodded sadly and went back down the stairs.

Lori felt his presence, knew Luke was there and that she had no reason to worry. He would save her and their child. He always knew what to do in a crisis, always knew the right thing to do for her. Her eyelids were heavy, and she moved her arm but felt pain so moved the other to cover her belly and her child.

"Lori? You awake, honey?"

She tried to say that she was, but only a croak emerged from between dry lips.

"Here, sip this." She felt the cool rim of a glass to her lips, and she drank, wanting more, but it was taken away too soon. "Only a little at a time, honey, or you'll be sick and lose it all. You can have a little more in a minute or two."

She nodded, licking the moisture over her lips, which felt cracked and rough.

"Did I lose our baby?"

"Doc isn't sure. The babe's still there, but you've been bleeding, and he isn't sure if you can carry to full term."

She heard his voice break and felt tears slip from between her lids and slide into her ears. She thought she nodded in acknowledgement but wanted to rage at the world that would harm her child, take away something so precious. She wouldn't accept the verdict.

"I'll carry to full term—this is our child we're

talking about. I will not lose our child."

She felt his hand cover hers on her stomach, and she knew their child was safe inside her. Would remain safe until it was time for it to be born.

She whispered, "It's a boy, you know."

"That sure, are you, or are you hedging your bet since there are only boys in the family?"

She could hear humor in his voice, humor and love.

"I was kinda set on a daughter," he said. "Beautiful, and sensitive, and sensible like her mother."

She felt his kiss on her forehead. "Maybe the next one, but this is a boy. Tough, opinionated, and all Foster. He will live through this. I can feel him giving me strength."

"I'm glad it's a boy then. The next three can be girls." She heard him hold his breath. She knew he was wondering if he had gone too far in his teasing.

"We'll just alternate until we get to seven. Even I don't think we can match the twelve your parents had in mind." She finally opened her eyes completely, taking in her husband who needed a shave and probably a supper.

He said unnecessarily, "I was so frightened when I found you outside like that. I lost a few years waiting for the doctor and got more gray hairs once I found the puncture marks."

"It was foolish of me. I didn't think what the sound was and kept moving. It all happened so fast."

"I know. I've run across many of them out in the pastures sunning themselves or getting water. Shoot them when we can because they take out cattle with a bite. You must be a very strong person to live through a bite like that. Leastwise that's what the doc says."

"It wasn't very big, so I hope that means it wasn't very poisonous."

"Let's not talk about it anymore. I'm going to let the others know you're awake and to send up some broth. Matt made some up for when you woke."

"I'd love some. Let the younger ones up to see me in case they're worried. Simon will be the most upset."

She saw him smile and called down to his brothers, anxious to let them know she was awake and wanting food. She noticed he was in clean clothes and his beard was scruffier than usual.

"Luke, how long have I been here?"

"You got bit on Tuesday, and this is Thursday evening." He seemed calm, but she knew better.

"I'm sorry I worried you."

"I'm glad you're awake now. Helen came by, and Sarah Ann brought bread and a cake for the boys. They both insisted on seeing you for themselves. Did you plan on Helen being your midwife?"

She licked her lips, and he returned to hold the glass for her again. After the drink, she could answer. "Yes, she has helped deliver most of the younger children here in town. Doc says he can't be everywhere at one time, so she handles the births unless they think it might need his expertise. She's very knowledgeable, and I trust her fully."

"Then so do I. Simon's waiting outside, can he come in?"

"Of course, I want to know how his book report went on *The Whale*."

The boy came in shyly. "Aw-w-w, I don't want to talk about school. I want to know how big the snake was, and what it sounded like, and if it hurt, and…."

Luke said, "Whoa, little brother. I let you come up here to see how much better she is, not to ask her a hundred questions."

The youngster looked at the man closest to a parent he had. "I just want to be able to tell the others at school all about it. Nobody else knows anyone who's been bit."

Lorelei felt it was time to intervene. "I will tell you what it was like, but do not make too big a story out of it. I was lucky Luke made it home in time to help me. Please make sure your friends know the dangers of getting bit, and maybe what to do if they or someone close is bitten."

The child nodded, and she saw Peter and Paul at the top of the stairs. She called to them, "You two may as well hear the gory details, so I won't need to keep repeating them." As she began the very unthrilling event, she nodded for Luke to go down, eat, and clean up. He nodded, but mouthed the words, "I love you" before leaving.

What a time to tell her. His first words of love in less than a whisper. She came back to reality when Simon asked to see the actual puncture marks, and she obliged, giving all the boys a chance to examine the purplish, swollen wound as if it were a new puppy.

The gray-haired man put his stethoscope away. "Well, little lady, this will be the last house call for us unless you go into labor."

Lorelei was grateful the danger to her unborn child was over. "Thank you, Doctor. I am so relieved to know my baby is safe inside me."

"Those venoms have something to do with

clotting of the blood, and with you so newly pregnant, those parts were easily attacked. Probably has something to do with the snake's usual victims, you know, to have them bleed to death." He expelled a deep sigh. "Anyway, no more gruesome thoughts for you."

"I have been thinking, though. Funny how all the Foster boys have the same blue eyes and dimples. I expect this one will, as well." She watched his expression to see if he would get there before she did. "I've always thought Helen's youngest children's hazel eyes are very distinctive—they're just like your hazel eyes."

He turned away putting something into the worn, black bag next to him. When he turned back, there was a sheen in his eyes. "I had been a widower for a couple of years when I started caring for her husband. Helen was trying so hard to be brave for him, take care of the frightened children, and keep the farm going, although it was a thankless job."

Lorelei remained silent letting the man choose his own words. Hopefully, it would help him find the right path.

"After her husband passed, I would stop by at the end of the day, presumably to check on the children and she would have me stay to supper. It gave me a reason to bring some provisions along with me. Told her if she'd cook, I'd think it fair. I didn't have anywhere else to be or anyone to go home to. It was pleasant to be with her." He appeared ashamed as he said the next. "I knew she was lonely too and things just changed between us. I asked her to marry me when she became pregnant with Caleb, but she refused. Said she couldn't marry so soon after the death of her husband."

"No one would have said anything about that. Not a woman with children to care for as well as a farm." She thought it sounded like something Helen would say, as if having a child without a husband wouldn't give people something to talk about. She also thought it was more about thinking the doctor wouldn't have asked her to marry him if she hadn't been expecting his child.

"I tried to tell her that, but she refused me repeatedly. After Caleb was born, the talk began, but she said she didn't care since what they said was the truth. Said she had been with a man she wasn't married to. I love her, and I didn't like her being talked about like that, but it didn't keep me away from her. We had Molly just a couple of years later."

"They are delightful children, and Helen is a good mother. Why don't you ask her again? I think you may be pleasantly surprised at her change of heart."

"You don't think she'll send me away with a flea in my ear? She was right angry the last time I brought the subject up."

"Try again. Keep trying because those children need a father as much as you need a family. Helen knows that as well. Besides, I believe she loves you just as much."

He nodded as he stood to leave. "She always said she wasn't meant to be a doctor's wife, and I wasn't meant to be a farmer. Maybe there's some middle ground there somewhere."

CHAPTER TWELVE

Lorelei was taking her first trip to town since her illness. Luke even loosened up enough to allow Matthew to do the driving since he needed to speak with the mayor's son. Some sort of legal paperwork Matt wanted done. She was simply glad to see her husband relaxing a little more and not watching her like a keg of explosives.

Matthew had been quiet, which was unlike him. He usually talked constantly, and if he hadn't anything to say, then would tease her just to keep words flowing.

She heard him clear his throat. "I've been trying to find the right time to tell you I'm leaving for Alaska. Not because I want to, but because I can't stay and watch you with him. When you almost died, I wanted to be the one to sit with you. It ate me up knowing you were having his child and probably became pregnant up at the mountain cabin."

Her heart sank at his words. She had hoped his emotions weren't involved. Hoped he had merely been having growing pains and would leave to make his own way in the world, choose his own destiny. She didn't want to be the reason the family was changing.

"Matthew, you shouldn't say these things—feel these things." She felt this wasn't really happening. She didn't want to hear his confession, didn't want to think how it would change the relationship between the two brothers and herself.

"Don't you think I don't know that? I want to physically hit something every time I think of that morning Luke brought you home. It could have been me. He wanted me to go into town to pick up those fence posts so he could see to something more important here at the ranch. But I got obstinate and told him if he needed fence posts for his ranch, he could fetch them himself. He met you instead of it being me."

"I don't think fate works that way. I don't think you envy Luke at all, but you do envy his being able to live the life he selected, he wants. I think your life lies in a different direction, and I don't mean just away from the farm, but away from Whitewater Rapids. I think you are destined to do great things."

He scoffed, snorting air out his nostrils in disdain.

Lorelei spoke sternly. "Listen to me when I tell you the way you work with wood is as an artist with paint, a sculptor with stone. You don't just nail and glue together pieces of wood. You make them appear as if they were meant to be together, as if they were nothing until you joined them. Your carving speaks for itself, images come to life. I expect that prairie dog to start barking every time I come into the parlor."

Quietly, he replied, "And all I could think of for days was that I would have to make your coffin without ever telling you how I feel. I even went to my workshop and designed a pattern for the top, something so everyone would know you are loved and missed by a family. I'm so glad I never had to actually build it, but I mourned your loss as if I had."

"Matthew, I don't know how to make this easier on you. You know my feelings for you, all the brothers, but I love Luke differently. Maybe I always knew I would."

"I can move on knowing I at least told you honestly why I'm leaving now. You're a lovely woman with a lovely heart, Lori. I'm going to miss you."

She leaned against his arm. "And I'm going to miss you. But remember, just because you leave home doesn't mean you aren't welcome back. That's what home means."

They rode silently the rest of the hour, both thinking. She hoped she had said the right things, the right words to ease his bruised heart. How was she ever going to handle more of them leaving if she couldn't let the oldest go?

When the two of them communed like this alone in their room, Lorelei felt the most at peace. Luke held her against his chest as their breaths calmed, saying, "I never thought love would be like this. So overwhelming I can't think of anything else. I can't go through that again. I can't be so focused on one that the others suffer." She knew her husband was still hurting, feeling he was losing control even days after the incident.

Lorelei tried to play down the event now that everyone was safe. "No one suffered, and this is what parents do all the time. They worry about the one who is ill or not doing well in school or is heartsick. When one worry is solved, another takes its place."

"I know how to help the boys. I lived through what they do, but not you. How do I make sure you're happy and that you won't leave me?"

She rolled over and gazed into his eyes as best she could with the lamp turned low. "I don't know why you think I'm not happy here with you and the boys. I love taking care of you, making sure there is food stored for our needs, making interesting suppers, even doing your laundry."

"But that's not what you were trained to do. You're educated, could have a fancy titled job in a big city."

She placed her hands on both sides of his face and kissed him. "No one asked me if I wanted to be a librarian. It was assumed because I grew up in one, helped my father every daylight hour with his work. I enjoyed the books, enjoyed reading about the many adventures, other people's lives. But I have a life here with you that is so much more rewarding. Why should I worry about a big, white whale? His story is written. I'm helping to make this one, the one we live. I don't want to be somewhere else doing something else. Do you?"

"No, but I was raised on the ranch, and this is all I ever wanted. Taking care of the boys and growing the herds. It's what I thought my life would be. A shadowy wife was in the future, but I thought she would be a plain-faced rancher's daughter. Now I wake up every morning to the most beautiful woman who is happy most of the time and tells me she is happy doing what she's doing. I have no complaints."

"But you do have reservations. You can't believe your luck. I'm telling you I would have it no other way. I don't want to think about later when the boys go their own way."

"Well, sure, the boys will get married, but we will chip in and build them each a house of their own somewhere on the property. Increase the herd to support us all…"

"No, Luke, I mean when they leave us, the ranch life. Some of them have other dreams. It doesn't mean they don't appreciate what you do or enjoy working alongside their brothers now. It does mean they have plans for their future other than ranching. That something else has entered their mind and their heart."

"They've said that to you? That they're unhappy here?" The concept seemed foreign to Luke. As if he'd never taken the possibility into his head.

"No one is unhappy, but they are still growing and maturing into young men who have different views of the world. I told you they love you, and if you insist they're needed, they will stay—and be miserable."

He nodded. "I see. My dream is increasing the herds, the pastures, while they may want what? To leave me and the ranch?"

"I know a few have expectations of leaving at some point. The twins for instance want to be engineers and design bridges and train trestles, anything having to do with suspension and tension and metal, and I don't know what all."

"How do you know these things?"

"From table talk, I guess. You and the older boys have a conversation about the ranch and what needs to be done the next day while the younger ones talk about what interests them.

"So, Simon wants to leave too?"

"Simon is undecided between being a lawyer and helping people or a doctor and healing people. Either way, the last three will be going on to university. It's something we need to plan on."

"You're unbelievable. No wonder I think you're so much better than I deserve. It's because you are hearing them, and I'm giving orders. Who else is leaving?" She felt his thumb rub her shoulder unconsciously.

"Um-m-m, Matthew aspires to become a wood carver, possibly furniture maker. Andrew is about to ask Sarah Ann to marry him and come and live on the ranch, and Bartholomew has been courting the neighbor's daughter. Her father has no sons and is hinting at offering the newlyweds the farm when he retires."

"Again, I had no idea. Of course, I should have guessed they would want wives as soon as they saw how lucky I was in getting mine." He pulled her head down to kiss her. She returned the kisses, thankful he was accepting all the possible changes in his life. Including becoming a father.

"Everyone's life changes. Helen is going to marry Doctor Hatch and give her youngest their rightful name. The town is in a rumor rage, but things will calm down after a while. The older children don't understand the uproar since they knew the doctor fathered their siblings. He was a visitor to their home and knew there was a relationship between him and their mother. Now things will be better since Helen is sure to accept more from him that will help the entire family."

"Didn't know the old man had it in him. I'm glad he finally decided to do the right thing."

"It was Helen who held back. I think she finally realized it was better to spend her life with him than pretend she didn't know him. After all, those youngest are going to be as easily recognized as the Foster brothers."

"I hope our little one has your eyes and smile. It's time we added some spice to the family line." He rolled her over laughing into her neck.

Lorelei wished for just the opposite and knew the Foster blue eyes and dimpled cheeks were going to bless her children like a kiss of an angel.

Matthew made his announcement at supper. It caused a ruckus among the brothers. All except Luke who watched his family through narrowed eyes. Lorelei watched Luke. She knew he would be hurt at what he would see as a defection, but it was the best for all involved.

Matthew needed to be his own man, not always looking to Luke for answers or orders. He needed to meet other women so he could put his feelings for her into proper perspective. He needed to find the world he wanted to rule.

Both Luke and Matthew refused to make eye contact with one another or with her. Interesting. Now she knew how it felt to be a bone between two rivaling dogs. She didn't want Matthew to leave like this. Too much could happen quickly, and if the men left one another's sides angry, then they might never meet again to work out the problems.

Luke opened the door off the main section of the barn to find Matt packing up his woodworking tools. Matt glanced behind him but returned to setting things in boxes and sacks.

"I knew I'd find you here, Matt. You always come here when you have something to work out." He saw the barren walls, which were usually full of tools and the diminished stack of boards. "So, you've been planning this for a while, but didn't warn me?"

"I waited until I felt it was the right time. You have Lori to back you up with the boys now. She can be your emotional rock. Andrew always wanted to be second-in-command of the ranch, and as I see it, he will be a married man as well. Time for him to build a cabin and be his own man, too."

Luke put out his hands as if to plead. "If it's the living with all your brothers that's bothering you, we can build two cabins almost as fast as one. Just tell me which piece of property you want for your own. We can work it out. You don't have to leave for me to give you the freedom to do what you want. I guess I was just so used to you all following my lead. I can change…" He dropped his hands in frustration as Matt slowly shook his head.

"It isn't anything you did, Luke. I have the utmost respect and pride for how you took on all the responsibilities at such a young age. I look at the twins and wonder how you did it all at their age. I think I was fooling myself thinking I could have done it just as well."

"You could have done it if you were the oldest. I wanted all of you to have as much of a childhood as you could. We all needed to work our share, but I wanted to take on the worry of paying taxes and making the whole thing pay. Some years it did and some years it didn't, but I didn't want the ranch's ups and downs to weigh heavily on the rest of you."

"It took me until recently to figure that out. You were protecting us from life, and I get that you wanted to do that, but I'm not that much younger than you. I could have taken on more of the burden."

"I agree now that you say it. I guess I got in such a

habit of working out problems on my own, not having anyone to talk it out with that's the only way I knew to do things."

"Until you married Lori. You are such a lucky son of a... I know you worry about her getting fed up with working so hard, mending and remending sheets and shirts. But trust me when I tell you, she loves being your wife. She loves you." He turned to sort through items in the crate before glaring back at him.

"I know—now. It took me a while to believe a man like me could luck into finding a beautiful, loving wife in the middle of a dusty street. Both of us covered with soot."

"Only you, brother, only you." His grin appeared furtively. "I don't mind telling you I would change places with you in a minute. Having a wife like Lorelei would be wonderful, but I have always thought of traveling. I just never thought to have the chance. I've seen the stories about the Alaskan Territory and how a man can make his way with hard work. Just like the original homesteaders, I'll take my place." He slapped Luke on the shoulder. "This is how it was meant to be, big brother. I've got traveling in my blood."

CHAPTER THIRTEEN

The whole family was there at the station to wave Matthew off to his new life in Alaska. He had a will drawn up, giving everything he owned to Luke in case he didn't return, but Lorelei didn't want to think of him never returning. He also signed over any rights to the ranch to Luke, so there would be no misunderstandings later.

Lorelei knew she would cry when the train pulled away, perhaps even before. The family she joined so short a time ago was already changing. As fast as her waistline. Matthew hugged her to him and then jumped apart laughing.

"Did my nephew just kick me? I felt it through all these clothes. He must be easy to sleep with at night." His smile was wide, and he seemed more relaxed than ever.

"Yes, I have been woken from a deep sleep more than once."

"Well, tell him about his handsome, wise Uncle Matt, won't you? I would hate for him not to know me."

"I'll read him the letters you've promised to write. I want to know all about Alaska, and I expect a carved polar bear to sit next to the prairie dog on the shelf." She heard the conductor call "all aboard" for a final time, and Matthew jumped onto the small platform as it went past.

Luke held her with his arm around her waist. She leaned into him for comfort, and he kissed her on the temple. "He'll be all right, Lori. He knows he can wire us for help if he needs it. He explained this is something he has always wanted to do. Every parent has to let their children grow and move on in life. We'll have plenty of practice by the time our little ones need to leave the nest. I hope at least one wants the ranch, but if not, I plan on lots of nephews as well."

Lorelei stared at her husband. "Don't you dare only think of the boys as ranchers, Luke Foster. I've heard of plenty of women who run large ranches. Our daughters and nieces may be interested, as well."

"Yes, sweetheart. I'm not used to thinking of females in the family since you insist you are carrying my son."

When they returned to the ranch, Lorelei let her tears flow as they walked into the kitchen and found a beautifully designed and crafted child's highchair. It glowed with a high shine, and the wood was satin smooth, so no little ones could get a sliver. The legs were turned spindles with flutes and decorative stretchers between the legs for support. There was an open area through the back to carry the chair one-handed while the other held a child. From the front, it looked like two hearts, and from the back, it was part of a design that read, "Foster's Future."

She rubbed her hand over the smooth surfaces. "Luke, he left us a part of him. The baby will use this until his sister bumps him out of it."

"Or we write and ask for another. He made a second cradle when the twins were born," Luke told her something Matthew had all those months ago.

Smiling bravely, she nodded. "Anything to remind him he has a family here that still misses him and wants him home."

Epilogue

Lorelei scooped the oozing apple sauce from her son's chin with the small spoon before offering it to him again. She wasn't thinking about her task, but about Matthew coming back from Alaska with his Russian bride. A bride he openly admitted to loving beyond measure. It piqued Lorelei's interest to meet this woman who could bring Matthew home to his family, if only for a visit.

Andrew and Sarah Ann came in with their new little one. The first girl in the Foster family for over two generations. The baby was so young she didn't appreciate the honor yet, but Lorelei was sure she would learn to hold it over the boys' heads soon enough.

"Luke not back with the prodigal son?" Andrew teased. He had taken Matthew's place as the family comedian.

"Married prodigal son, remember, Andrew. The train might be a little late, and I made a meal that would hold if need be," she told the couple.

Sarah Ann placed a spice cake on the counter. "Smells delicious as usual, Lorelei. I never resent having to eat over here especially since Grace was born."

Andrew added, "I'll eat without them, and they can have leftovers. Where are the others?"

"All three younger ones went in the back of the wagon. Said they couldn't wait to see their big brother."

"I'm their big brother, too, and I never receive more than a wave when I show up," Andrew commented.

"You live less than a quarter of a mile away, and they see you most days working with the herd. This is different." She tried to ease any resentment if there was any between the two siblings.

"I understand. I'm excited to see him again, too. It's been only a little over two years, and I must admit I missed his wit and his calmness in the most upsetting of times. I would follow him out to the woodworking room, and the sound of his hasp or sandpaper would sooth me. Made me wish I had the talent to do the same." He walked to his wife and put his arm around her waist pulling her close to his side.

"Well, that's the wagon now, so if you two are ready, I'm going to grab Jacob, and we'll meet his uncle on the front porch." She untied the belt holding her son in his chair and carried him with her.

She spotted Matthew wearing a Russian-style fur hat with the most exquisite woman sitting next to him. The woman appeared petite to his height and had the appearance of fragility, but something about her mouth and eyes made Lorelei think she was as strong as the ice floes.

Jumping down, Matthew raised his arms to take his wife's waist and lifted her gently to the ground. He practically pushed her to the porch to introduce her to Lorelei.

"My favorite sister-in-law, may I present my wife, Natasha." Then, seeing Andrew right behind with his wife, added, "Sorry, I'm not used to all the changes since I've been gone. Sarah Ann is my sister-in-law now, too. Maybe I need to introduce Lori as my oldest sister-in-law…"

Andrew bent down to help the bride up the stairs saying, "Best stop while you're ahead, brother. I'm Andrew, evidently the most sophisticated brother here at the moment and this is my wife, Sarah Ann, and daughter, Grace."

Natasha had a sweet voice and an intriguing accent. Lorelei could tell the younger boys were in love immediately. "I have heard of all of you. It is all that Matthew talked about on the ship here."

"Come in, all of you, please." Lorelei waved them all inside waiting for her husband to unload the trunks and send Peter to the barn with the team.

"Well, are you sorry you chose me?" Luke asked, as he came to her side and tickled Jacob under his chin.

She tipped her head and received a long kiss not merited by the relatively short time apart. "I never had a doubt I chose the right Foster from the first time under those buffalo skins."

He tried to push into the hip not taken up by their son. "Why in the world did you mention those? Now I'll have to wait to reward you for hours." He kissed her passionately again.

"It's just as long for me. Now let's go in and try to concentrate on the family being back together. I see Bartholomew and Fanny driving in the gate right now."

"I will, but don't think me rude if I disappear upstairs with you early. I'm the rancher, you know, and we get up early in the morning." He waggled his brows and she laughed along with their son at Luke's antics.

A word about the author...

have been reading as far back as I can remember.

I write historical romance - Medieval, Highland, Georgian, Regency and my favorite Western US.

I remind my husband he is still my hero and even after 50 years together still takes my breath away.

www.authorsusanpayne.com